T0274802

The Unsaddled

SEAGULL BOOKS
•
CELEBRATING
40 YEARS

THE FRENCH LIST

PASCAL QUIGNARD

The Unsaddled

TRANSLATED BY JOHN TAYLOR

LONDON NEW YORK CALCUTTA

**PAP
TAGORE**

www.bibliofrance.in

The work is published with the support of the
Publication Assistance Programmes of the Institut français

Seagull Books, 2023

First published in French as *Les désarçonnés*
© Editions Grasset & Fasquelle, 2012

First published in English translation by Seagull Books, 2023
English translation © John Taylor, 2023

ISBN 978 1 80309 150 1

British Library Cataloguing-in-Publication Data
A catalogue record for this book is available from the British Library

Typeset by Seagull Books, Calcutta, India
Printed and bound by WordsWorth India, New Delhi, India

CONTENTS

He was vomiting blood. The crows were alighting, in front of his window, on the pointed roof of the Louvre. They flocked together there in a great multitude. The King of France was afraid of these birds swarming on the roof tiles, each bird pushing out with its wings a place for itself among the others, cawing, squawking, cheeping, shrieking. The King thought that those gleaming, glistening sharp little heads were the souls of the dead reproaching him for the massacre to which he had consented on the day when the whole city was celebrating Saint Bartholomew's Day. If he kept lying down, he would start suffocating and end up coughing blood. So he got up. Every night, he would go to one of the windows several times and see if the birds had had the good idea to fly away. Only twenty-four years old, he looked like an old man. On the night of 28 May 1574, in one of the palace rooms, Ruggieri had himself helped by two monks. They set up an altar. They covered it with a black cloth. They placed two candlesticks on it, with black candles. They went off to fetch a chalice full of the blood that the King had vomited a little earlier in the evening. In front of the altar, very close to the altar, they had Charles IX sit down on a stool. Catherine de' Medici settled in an armchair, next to him, and she was the one who gave the order to begin. One of the monks showed in a young Jewish catechumen. Ruggieri had him kneel in front of him. He asks him to open his mouth and stick out his tongue; he places the consecrated white host on the young man's tongue for the first time; the child has barely closed his mouth over the body of the Lord when a guard beheads him with his sword. A monk picks up the head; he sets it on the black host in front of the chalice full of blood that has been placed on the altar. Ruggieri tells the King of France to approach, to bend his own head down towards the mouth of the child (the newest Christian, the most recent death), to bring his ear very close to his lips while beckoning him to say what will happen in times to come. After a brief silence, the lips of the cut-off head utter a murmur. The child's lips say 'I am forced to' twice, distinctly, without anyone understanding very well the meaning of these words. However, just after these words have been said, the King of France faints. Catherine de' Medici squats alongside her son and has him sniff smelling salts. When he regains consciousness, Charles IX points to the head of the dead child and shouts: 'Take this thing away from me!' Two days later, on 30 May 1574, the King suffocates in his blood, groaning with terror, while the Queen Mother rocks him.

I pushed the shop door in Bergheim. The interval that rings is a third. I say:

'Ludwig, have you received the bottles of schist wine?'

'You're in a tobacco shop here, Herr Chenogne, and my name is Albrecht.'

I thanked him by using his new first name and prudently closed the door.

The Absence

Coming back from a military mission to Aranjuez, Ferdinand VII, Prince of the Asturias, offered a marvellous horse to George Sand's father. It had a magnificent coat. It was young and, as it were, untameable. Its name was Leopardo.

On Friday, 17 September 1808, George Sand's father rode Leopardo from Nohant to La Châtre to play in a quartet at the Duverret's. He dined there, perfectly fulfilled his violinist's role, and left them at eleven o'clock. The horse, which had started to gallop when leaving the bridge, ran into some stone rubble in the darkness, almost rolled over and straightened up so violently that its rider was thrown off the saddle and back ten feet from there. The vertebrae in the rider's neck were broken. George Sand's father was thirty-one years old. He was laid out on an inn table. The dead man was carried on this table, with a lantern held out in front of him to see in the darkness, all the way to Nohant. The four-year-old child was awakened. She had been sleeping and was told that her father had been thrown off his horse.

*

Fatherless, the child of a scorned, half-insane servant woman, the granddaughter of an old, sick, aristocratic woman (rich as Croesus, with a smothering sadness to her, excellent musician), Aurore, when she became an adolescent, in despair at having been torn away from the peaceful convent where she had been happy, suddenly, 'twenty feet of water in the Indre river' attract her.

The 'vertigo of death', she writes, engulfs her as soon as she sees water. She rushes into what engulfs her. She drowns.

It's her horse, whose name is Colette, that saves her by swimming, by pushing her with its nostrils and teeth towards the shore.

The adolescent grasps a 'pollarded willow'.

All her life, George Sand clutches a 'pollarded willow'.

She writes: 'It wasn't my fault that I was tempted to die. More than a pistol, more than laudanum, it was especially water which, like a mysterious charm, attracted me. I would no longer stroll anywhere except along the banks of streams until I had found a deep spot. Then, stopping along the edge, it was if I were bound by a magnet.'

*

It's not George Sand's need to withdraw as far away as possible from family members, from servants, from the group, to take shelter in a corner of space, which strikes me as an extraordinary aspiration, but, rather, the name that she gave to this shelter: she called it 'the absence'.

5

She didn't say otium, study, private room, solitude. She called this 'little corner' of her house in Nohant: The Absence.

All her life, she will wish to be absent inside The Absence.

It happens that, every time she found herself in Nohant, George Sand wrote in the bedroom where, when she was a child, her father's death from being thrown off the saddle was announced to her. It was there that they had her put on black socks. It was there that the naked little four-year-old body was shrouded in a heavy silk dress too big for her. It was in that bedroom that the little girl had been forced to wrap up her hair in a widow's black veil. It is in this room that, for her entire life, she waited for her father 'to finish being dead'.

*

On 23 July 1856, George Sand writes to Charles Poncy: 'I always aspire to The Absence. The only life that suits me is absence, the life of reflection.'

More than ten years later (on 11 January 1867), George Sand writes to Gustave Flaubert: 'I lose all interest in anything that is not my little ideal of peaceful work. My brain no longer progresses except from synthesis to analysis. In the past, it was the opposite. At present, what presents itself before my eyes when I awake is the planet. I have some difficulty in finding the ego, which once interested me, on it.'

All one's life, one seeks the place of the origin, the place before the world, that is, the place where the ego can be absent and the body forget itself.

CHAPTER 4

All children find in the example of those who conceived them the model of their unhappiness. Whence the strange structure of belatedness that affects human time, especially in well-educated industrial societies keen on technical novelty, where studies are prolonged well beyond puberty. The suffering for which young people ready themselves attracts them like an increasingly insubstantial and, to their eyes, incomprehensible memory. Without knowing it, they near those who have stopped living for a long time, passing on ways of being that they have merely glimpsed. They are already old without perceiving it. Their hell is the torch shining on them, whereas they see only light. Only a pain remains, yet whose plaint has become merely sonorous; they barely hear it as it is transmitted from age to age, imperceptibly, in the form of their patronymic.

*

As it happens, my father, my two grandfathers, and most of my great grandfathers fought in the three successive Franco-German wars.

On 19 July 1870, on 3 August 1914 and on 3 September 1939, three general mobilizations took place on both sides of a border that was once again shifting.

In my family, we no longer knew when we were German, when we were French. Beginning in 842, Strasbourg. Beginning in 843, Verdun. Beginning in 867, Metz. Borders are lines—imaginary, moving, cruel, ancestral. Frontlines where the battle takes place, lines full of archaeological deposits of weapons, horses, mass graves, anxieties. Imaginary lines of doubt and bereavements.

*

We call vendetta an exchange of dead people even as we call marriage an exchange of women. And every dead person in this case is even more so a marriage, in that at the end of a genuine vendetta, the wife and children of he who has been murdered are abducted in compensation for a previous murder. This is how I was raised by a young woman, by an adult woman, by an old woman.

Cäcilia, Anne, Marie.

Müller, Bruneau, Estève.

In humanity, if everything is symmetry, this is because language symmetrizes everything.

In animal societies, everything is asymmetry: everything is predation. The relationship between wild animals is defined by aggression without reciprocity. In the animal world, there is not the slightest war. Individuality is extreme there. Identity, gender, generality, the opposition that backs them up, are born only among human beings.

Thus, it is language alone—the child's acquisition of the language of the group that precedes him, the simple functioning of this language that he struggles to make his own—which makes everything that is different become opposed, reciprocal, polarized, sexual, passionate, jealous, hostile, warlike, enemy.

*

God says: Meliores sumus singuli. We are better when isolated. We are alone by origin. One slips one's head into The Absence. Padlocking the iron-rail gate, locking the door, closing the window, we expect that outside, very far away, the pogrom will go by without spotting us.

Sumus singuli.

It is not judicious to pursue one's parents' wishes. It is inopportune to follow the wishes of the group. May nothing transfer onto your head. Flee from transfers. Stop serving. 'Everywhere hate is primary' means 'Everywhere solitude is preferable'.

Seneca wrote: Become exauctoratus. Word for word: 'Become dis-enlisted as a gladiator.' 'Exauctoro' is a performative verb that means: 'I give leave to a soldier.' Pronounced by the emperor when shows take place, the word means: 'I free the gladiator from arena servitude.' 'I free the gladiator from arena service' means 'I relieve this man from death at the end of a combat.'

Become ex-authorized.

Verba exauctorata are words out of service.

Become a word out of service.

Authorize yourself to abandon your patronymic so that it will resemble a word out of service on your lips.

*

Most human beings are divided between chaos and defence against chaos.

Almost all of us are cut in half. On one side, dementia; on the other, the code.

Rabbi Loeb is much more radical: For the road that allows one to cross human life is a razor blade. On one side, hell; on the other side, hell.

First of all, there are two roads. Coitus brings them together. Then there are three roads. It is at birth that they split. King Laios was standing on a chariot driven by two mares. He was killed at the fork of three paths, in Phocis, where the path coming down from Daulis met up with the path leading to Delphi. Oedipus drove ten wild horses in front of him. The road that went up to Delphi is much too narrow for them to go up in a row.

*

Efface the happy roles among those in this world! Tolle felices! We will never believe ourselves to be unhappy if we eliminate the happy ones!

＊

Winnicott described the resentment that neurotic people feel when they encounter attractive faces. All bodies enchanted with being alive make them feel uneasy. They experience loathing when they encounter lively or bouncy souls. A more vindictive divergence than that of the poor against the rich. The irremissible war of the illiterate against men and women of letters. To slight, unhappy people, everything appears arrogance. Not at any price does a sick person want his faithful, pronominal illness to abandon him; he would feel much more reassured if everyone else's health were as problematic as his. Not at any price does an ugly person want his weight or his unsightliness to vanish; he wants beauty to be destroyed and slimness or slenderness to vanish from the surface of the earth.

CHAPTER 5

The Packsaddle of Shame

They bore above their heads spurts of sperm that had petrified.

In the Neolithic period, stags, which fled from human beings and were runaways by principle, ever untameable, unsociable in the very depths of their souls, came above horses in the hierarchy of wild animals because their beauty appeared irresistible. This precedence was unbearable to the vanity of horses, which would fight with stags until late at night. They would fight with them in the centre of clearings, regularly, every November.

An indecisive duel.

In the clearing, at night, under the moon, every hour, the neighing horse would leap towards the sky.

The stag would bell in the shadows, tossing his sperm into the void.

With every assault, the antlers would push back the mane.

The belling would drive the neighing out of the dark forest, towards the plain.

At daybreak, the stag would go off to drink at a hidden source, in the middle of the forest, beneath the weight of the darkest antlers.

Meanwhile, the magnificent horse would be grazing on the grass at the edge of the forest, in the dawn sunlight, its coat covered with water.

Then, coming from the valley, the man approached. He was carrying a leather whip in his left hand. He reached out his right hand. He softly caressed its flank with his fingers, saying to the horse, murmuring in its ear:

'I will offer you the victory if you let me put myself on your back.'

The horse agreed, hoping to conquer the stag.

The centaur won.

The stag was beheaded.

In French, the cut-off head of the stag is called a massacre.

However, after this triumph, the horse could no longer get rid of the rider, nor of the bit to which he had given its teeth, nor of the riding crop that wounded its belly. The horse turned to the elated, haughty, smug, smiling man, who was holding out a piece of sugar. Like all horses, its face showed an inexpressible sadness. The horse resigned itself for millennia. It eats the sugar, so as not to be stupid in addition to being subservient. The horse muses to itself: 'There are bad victories.'

*

Horace adds: However beautiful a horse is, it carries the packsaddle of shame. Look instead at stags! Endlessly growing above their faces full of pride is a superior virility, hard like wood, fascinating like a crown, ornately penned like a mysterious letter, soft like velvet. Now listen to horses! Everything that neighs is full of shamelessness and whininess. It is probably ever since its defeat that the stag flees human beings as hastily as it does horses. It can be said of the stag that it is fleeing made animal, but this fleeing is perhaps, behind this defeat, something very different from the victory won by the centaur: a strange triumph. An insubordination. Non-domestication exhibited, being-unsaddled-ness personified. It spends its time living in the forest of the world, tossing out its sperm into the winter, making use of its hours as it wishes, returning to the most secret place, hiding near the source where it remains nestled.

✳

One must flee. One must flee human beings. One must flee the policeman riding his horse and brandishing his white stick that vigorously hits the backs of workers, students, young women, children, crowds of people.

One must flee all the horses of the Military Supply Train.

One must never think that one is the strongest once one is alone.

Once a group starts yelling, at the bottom of a street, one must climb onto the roof, walk carefully across the tiles and protect oneself behind chimneys. One must flee not only all weapons but also the law, for if the defence is dependent on the attack, anything that intends to defend is in the service of this dependence. One must flee magistrates, lawyers, for this is the second packsaddle of shame. No human being will be able to put forth a defence that can be victorious. At the very instant that it seems to triumph over its adversary, the defence has consented to the risk of losing.

Once one has consented to the risk of losing, one has lost.

On playgrounds, it was already said: 'He who excuses himself accuses himself.'

Indeed, this was true.

In front of the man torturing you, you must never confess, because as soon as he has obtained your confession, he will eliminate you, because you are the witness of the means used to obtain your confession.

In front of a man who is accusing, you must not present a defence, because your justification imprisons you just as soon as a subject who acknowledges the fault for which he is threatened even as it legitimizes the law applied to him.

Thesis. A prey must never turn over his lot to its predators.

Scholium. Because the attack regulates the defence, because it subjugates one to a given time, because it enslaves one to a piece of ground, because it abides by the momentary configuration of the forces, one must know how not to succumb to the desire to rush headlong into the disadvantage of handing over the reins to domination and prematurely offering one's body to death.

*

Then the prince left his wife's bed, stepped over the body of his child, left his palace, fled. At the very instant he went through the gate of the castle wall, he became Buddha.

*

'The Bodhisattva always avoided questions, responding vacuously, in the void.'

One must know how to enter the heart of the forest, reach the fountain that the old language, long ago, simply called the 'font'.

One must know how to respond vacuously, in the void. This gives rise to books. One must know how to get lost in the void. This is the light in which we read them. One must respond to others only by creating. One must drop all other forms of replies. General Carl von Clausewitz wrote to Mainz: 'Never structure oneself like the adversary.' Never submit oneself to an incurable hostility and to the feeling of helplessness that causes you to pay attention to the hostility.

Creating means assailing a battlefront without a rival, where there is no community.

Creating is the only *good piece of ground* in the world.

For this 'ground' that suddenly surges forth in the eyes of one who creates does not exist before it is created.

This space where the book is created cannot be found in reality. It is unimaginable within symbolism. It is empty. This occasion cannot be anticipated by those who are envious of the happiness that they do not possess, by those who are thirsty for the blood of others, by those who unremittingly seek to devour the prey that they see escaping from them. For they do not invent their space in space and do not find the blood that they love in it.

CHAPTER 6

Solidarity Is Evil

There is a solidarity associated with evil. It is possible that solidarity, which relays gregariousness, is essentially bad because it is essentially nasty. Wolves fell in with human beings. Following the example given to them by wolves that came from eastern Asia, before those that they called dogs, and since wolves massed up whenever putting their prey to death and eating death, human beings began hunting in packs.

If one must disengage oneself from the worst, the virtue will always be forsakenness, being hollowed out, emptiness, fragmentation, indivi-dualization, asceticism.

Augustine: *Quid sunt regna nisi magna latrocinia?* What are realms? Vast acts of robbery. *Parva regna*, small realms: scavenging and plundering. For thieves are compelled by a social pact, the *pacto societatis*, to wrangle over prey, the *praeda*. Conflict, class struggle, civil war—such is the rule of social interaction, the *pactus societatis*.

*

It's not for nothing (*frustra*) that you wished many deep and mysterious (*opaca et secreta*) pages to be written: don't those *forests* also have their stags taking shelter, reassuring themselves, grazing, sleeping, ruminating there?

So speaks Augustine at the beginning of Book XI of his *Confessions*, addressing himself to God. He doesn't write *books*, as he says with an incomparable force, he writes *forests*.

Secret, opaque pages where the world before mankind still finds a place to wander and take shelter within a kind of night, beneath a kind of antlers.

Stag antlers that one also calls 'woods' (bois) in French.

Forests before cities.

Stags before wolves, dogs, and human beings.

Ruminatio before language.

Old Eden, antiquity of water, ancestral jungle before the celestial city.

*

Melanie Klein: War is an internal problem of mankind because for every combat, from the moment it is real, the more atrocious it gets, the more it takes on a healer's role. Every real danger pacifies anxiety, whatever its nature is, be it symbolic, imaginary or insane. War is the ghastly paradise of human societies.

The Silling Castle walls up the primitive scene.

Mass war is the continuous, normalizing, normed, referent regime of constituted societies. Order is always a battle order. The ceremony of power is always hierarchical. Social bonds can be interpreted only in terms of a power struggle. Power struggles are the alcoholized, as it were, pleasures of the head office. Politics is war (high-ranking officers, soldiers, instructors, sentinels) carried on by other means that are not more pacific (magistrates, policemen, youth workers, guards).

Michel Foucault: Power is in charge of defending society.

Power takes charge of reproduction (controlling the sexuality of women). Of reinforcing production (organizing the death of prey). Of increasing the pleasure of dominating among those in power (the power to give life or death). It tends to diversify without limits the hierarchical organization to increase the reign (the harnessing of wealth by a few people or by a single person).

The subjection is perpetuated by normalizing subjects, excluding the rebellious, educating small children, domesticating savages, letting war enslave, humiliating everyone and internalizing all that is penitential.

*

Power is even more linked to ceremony and sexual domination than to fraudulent profit and police blunders.

Ceremony defines violence in its intense state: violence that fascinates.

Why have women always been raped in all the wars, past or present? Because social reproduction *is* sexuality.

*

In Paris, on Thursday, 16 July 1942, at four in the morning, the operation titled 'Spring Breeze' begins. If power is a 'demonstration of power,' then the 'seizure of power' begins. The French police ring the doorbells of 27,361 Jews in the poorest parts of Paris (the 9th, 19th, and the 18th arrondissements). French policemen, obeying orders signed by the Prefect of Police, make 13,152 arrests. These arrests, made in plain daylight, with busses, in a velodrome, are *ceremonies* in which terror fascinates the group that dies without understanding anything, and projects its hold over the astonishment of the saved group looking on.

*

Queen Medea: Sacra letifica appara! Prepare the death ceremony! In every instant of time, all the dead from the past form a mere prelude to the theme that will emerge.

*

Claude Simon rode to war on a horse, on the Belgian front. It is May 1940. Holding the reins in his left hand, he receives the order to brandish his sword in his right hand against the airplanes.

*

Sigulf the Warrior recalled the other era standing behind History.

The scene takes place at the very beginning of *The History of the Franks*.

Gregory of Tours writes in *Historia Francorum* IV, 47: King Clodoveccus (Clovis), after he had seized Touraine and Poitou, which belonged to Sygiberthus (Sigebert), withdrew to Bordeaux. Just as soon, Sigebert ordered Sigulf to go and dislodge him. At the head of his cavalry, Sigulf tracked him down and Clovis' army was forced to flee. Then Sigulf received from Sigebert the order to humiliate the King of France by having his knights chase after him *as if he were a wild beast at bay*. Sigebert said that the King of France needed to be 'halloed'. Then that the hunting horns must be sounded as a sign of mockery (ludibrium). But Clovis, managing to withdraw into Anjou, drew pride from this ludibrium. He took advantage of this halloing as if it were a coronation. King Clovis boasted in front of the assembly of his kindred that he had been treated like a *stag*.

CHAPTER 7

In 1526, King François I, upon his return from captivity in Madrid, promulgated the edict giving the King of France the exclusive right to hunt stag.

CHAPTER 8

I must confess that, whenever I sped on my tricycle into the Saint-Roch Square in Le Havre, I would enter, while singing my head off, the mass grave of the Second World War, which the municipality had covered over with flowers.

The sea wind constantly swept over the dock.

My little wooden raft, called Kon-Tiki, would take off as soon as I had placed it on the water. It was light as the cork from which it was made. It didn't discover Oceania: it rushed towards the brand-new concrete wall, where it would remain stuck because of the force of the squall.

Every morning, towards the end of night, not very awake, my stomach queasy, unhappy, I would progress as slowly as I could, leaning into the wind, my right hand holding the old leather briefcase that my mother had acquired in Boston in the 1930s, dragging my feet, trudging through the debris to the lycée in ruins, climbing up on the ruins, looking for marvels that were each time unpredictable, chasing off seagulls, rooks, field mice, spiders, rats, heading around the smashed-open walls, trampling on the rubble. More houses and churches remained standing in Guernica, the little Biscay town, in May 1937, than in the harbour of Le Havre in 1944. I had two brothers. The black pellet gun was my other brother, the transparent pellet gun, me, and the red pellet gun was my little brother. We slept in the same bedroom in a new building, constructed by Perret, that rose in the middle of a vast field of ruins, rubble, deconstructions, reconstructions, at the end of which could be seen the sea. We could see only the smokestacks and high bridges of the ocean liners that were coming back from the Americas and that made their sirens wail, waiting for the tugboats that would guide them into the port by pulling on their cables, before anchoring them on the thick bollards of the stone wharves dating back to Louis XIII. These tugboats were called *abeilles* (bees).

CHAPTER 9

The Lancelot Childhoods

Ruins—so begins *Lancelot*. Smoking ruins. His father, King Ban, has died. And the father has died, in front of the nursling, while he was watching the castle that he loved burn, while watching the churches cave in, while watching the minster collapse. The King feels such a violent pang of anguish that he falls off his horse, blood flows from his ears, and he has just time enough to turn his face towards the east. The Queen forgets her baby and rushes over to help her husband. At this tragic moment, all the horses of the retinue bolt out of line. Little Lancelot ends up lying under the hooves of the roussin horse that was carrying his firmly harnessed cradle.

Then, at just the moment when the child is nearly killed, the Lady of the Lake emerges at his side. She saves the orphan from the trampling horse. She lifts him to her chest. She hugs him against her soft breast. She sinks with him into the water, without uttering a word, to educate him about the mute mores of her realm.

One day, his penis erect, the handsome adolescent boy comes back up to the surface of the water; he begins by killing his tutor and leaves. Lancelot leaves. This defines him.

He leaves. That's all.

Leaving suffices.

Lancelot does not want to inherit his father's realm.

To reigning wisely he prefers wandering insanely. Going beyond the walls. Going through the gate. Fleeing the court. Riding his horse over the heath. Meeting as often as possible, in secret, another man's queen—who, as far as she is concerned, is unfaithful to King Arthur, her husband.

A few very rare times, the lovers denuded their bellies in front of each other.

Once, twice, they embraced in the bailey.

'You mustn't know my name!' Lancelot mysteriously declares to all the knights whom he encounters on his path.

The 'face from times past' of Lancelot in the forest is Aeneas on the sea.

*

In *The Lancelot Childhoods*, Lancelot declares:

'If a man becomes dependent on a single human being, he does nothing else but tremble.'

This is how Lancelot defines the experience of love. Unique, infinite dependence. Lancelot was the first knight who stuck a banderole on his helmet. To the extent that he is the secret queen's lover, he is the incognito knight. To the extent that he is the incognito knight, he needs to agree on a secret sign with Guinevere.

He is the lunar hero.

He keeps changing shape, place, 'signalization' in the nightly space.

He abandons the site for the sign.

He is the hero who periodically disappears so that his liaison remains nameless and can stay safe from language and being put to death.

'Lord,' Gawain asks him, 'for pity's sake, tell me who you are.'

'No.'

'I beg you.'

'No, my Lord. I shall not say who I am.'

Even to Gawain, Lancelot replies: 'No. I will not say my name.' In all the novels dealing with him—which, in fact, only bring forth the matter behind his name because Lancelot is, literally, *lance d'or*, golden lance—Lancelot suddenly slips away. Such are *The Lancelot Endings*. Either he vanishes into a hermitage (he is fifty-five years old at the time). Or he is swallowed up in a jail in which he is imprisoned. He has stopped being outside. The golden lance has been broken. The quest is finished. King Arthur himself is dead. He has been buried in the Black Chapel. Torrential rains blur vision, the world is sad, the earth has become a wasteland.

CHAPTER 10

The First Language

If the hunting of quarry and spoils stands behind power, what cry stands behind language?

Frederick II of Sicily, who had made himself King of the Romans in 1215, became King of Jerusalem in 1229.

The King of Jerusalem tore away from ten mothers, who had previously been gagged, ten chubby nurselings when they emerged from the vulva.

He placed the ten babies in an entirely silent place so that mankind could learn what was the first language spoken at the origin. Because the King of Jerusalem wanted to discover what had been the 'language that had lived in God's mouth' before he created nature.

What language had God taught to Adam, in the Garden of Eden, at the end of the week?

The ten babies, fed, kept warm, cared-for, washed, living in the most total silence, died at the same time in the most total silence.

The King thus concluded that there was no language at the origin and no culture before nature.

The first language of mankind lay in dead silence.

CHAPTER 11

The Hero Who Cannot Be Unsaddled

Some people cannot be unsaddled. But theirs is perhaps an unenviable lot. In his *Dialogoi Nekrôn* 150, Lucian shows Arsaces impaled by a sarissa on his horse like a butterfly by a needle on a cork. Arsaces died on the banks of the Araxes during the last battle against the Cappadocians. Here is how he met death: a Thracian foot soldier, with his knee on the ground, was holding out his lance, and it ran through the breast of the charging horse, ran through Arsaces' groin, through his buttocks, the bronze point emerging from his back and transfixing both man and horse as a single entity. He was the first preserved centaur. Arsaces was the first rider who would ride his horse forever among the dead.

CHAPTER 12

Madame de Clèves

The Prince of Clèves got off his horse.

He handed the reins to his valet, at the corner of the rue du Chaume.

This is where Monsieur de Clèves came across his wife, one evening, while Saint-Mégrin was embracing her.

The lovers, however, did not hear the prince coming up behind them. The Prince of Clèves grasped Saint-Mégrin, who was completely naked and astride his wife, seized his arms, cried out for his servants who grabbed the man's four limbs and lifted him. In this way, by lifting him, they tore Saint-Mégrin's penis from Madame de Clèves' abdomen. Monsieur de Clèves then turned to his wife, who was terror-stricken on the bed, and shouted at her to keep her eyes wide open. She opened her eyes wide. Then Monsieur de Clèves ordered his servants to throw Saint-Mégrin out the window. Completely naked, Saint-Mégrin was yelling as they threw him out the window. He floated in the air.

Down he dropped.

Then Madame de Clèves silently buried her face in her hands.

Monsieur de Clèves ordered his valets to go down to the street and finish off Saint-Mégrin with knives on the cobblestones if he had managed to survive the defenestration. The Connétable de Clisson's mansion was next door. The Connétable and his people witnessed the scene. We witness the scene. Those who read witness the scene. It is endless. Every recounted scene is engraved in those who do not see it and they see it without seeing it and it is repeated in dreams and is disseminated during the day. As I spend my afternoons wandering around Paris, in the pedestrian streets, in the bicycle lanes, in dead-ends, in slums, in industrial wastelands, in the back lots of closed-down factories, alongside bins where embarrassed old men or women furtively push a shopping caddy full of bags, rummaging to find something to sell on the sidewalks, to find something to eat, everywhere I seek those old cobblestones stained with blood; everywhere I find them; everywhere one puts one's foot down on memories; one slips on memories; one stumbles on memories; one tumbles down into memories; one collapses into memories; children stick their fingers into their mouths; they enjoy putting their forefingers wet with saliva on the dull burning metal of the zinc drainpipe; the trace quickly vanishes in the sunlight. This is how blood disappears in the History of the men who make it flow. But teeth grow back. Fingernails grow back. Claws grow back. The *door is open*. 'The door is open!' was Epictetus' maxim. Epictetus lived in Rome at the end of the first century after Jesus, as the slave of a slave. Epictetus' maxim means: 'Kill yourself when you want to! Nature holds a door forever open to your body as long as it has the power to breathe, to run, to leap! Kill yourself as soon as you suffer!'

CHAPTER 13

Epictetus

I find one sentence by Epictetus extraordinary because it is unpredictable in the development of its consequences. It belongs to Book II, Chapter XXIII, paragraph 16: A disciple can be superior to his master even as a dog can be better than the hunter, a stag than the dog chasing it, a horse than the rider, an instrument than the musician, subjects than the king.

CHAPTER 14

The Unsaddled

In 1577, Agrippa d'Aubigné fell off his horse. He is covered by three corpses. Left behind as dead, gathered up as a corpse among other corpses, he is tossed onto a cart. A soldier suddenly sees his torso rising; he is extirpated from the pile of dead men; he is washed; his wounds are cleansed and bandaged. He is carried and laid out on a bed. Then, regaining consciousness, Agrippa d'Aubigné hastily dictates to the Elder of the small town the first lines of the *Tragiques* 'as a testament'.

Later, still stuck in bed, he will write, in a letter, that he had composed the first hundred lines of the *Tragiques* during 'sequences of suffering'.

When the time comes to publish the entire poem, he uses four enigmatic letters as a penname: LBDD. They mean *le bouc du desert* (the billy goat of the desert).

*

It was not on the day after his castration, in 1118, that Abelard began to draft the story of his misfortunes. It was twelve years later, after his horse accident in 1129 and during the year that followed. It was not in France, but in

Brittany. He fell off the horse badly, violently hitting his head while he was riding off from his priory of Saint Gildas de Rhuys to go to Nantes. The cervical vertebrae are dislocated. He screams. He is transported back to the priory. He writes *Historia calamitatum*.

*

One day, at the beginning of the era, the high priest of the Temple of Jerusalem entrusts Saul with six letters to take to the synagogue in Damascus.

The Roman citizen, a fundamentalist Jewish radical cleric from Tarsus, rides his horse all day long.

Suddenly (in Greek, *exaiphnès*), a light falls from the sky. This light envelops him in brightness and he falls from his horse.

He is lying on the ground, on his back, between the hooves of his horse, in the middle of this light.

He abandons his name, Saul, for that of Paul.

*

Saint Paul, Abelard, Agrippa d'Aubigné begin to write because they have fallen off a horse.

At least they begin to write because they have the impression of coming back from the world of the dead.

Like all men and women during the ecstatic trembling at the end of the trance, their bodies fall backwards.

The *situation renversante*, the situation that throws one backwards, that overturns one, refers to the moment when the shamanic journey begins.

It is like a second birth opening out during one's lifetime.

In Agrippa d'Aubigné's case, it is truly a second birth. For birth is inscribed in his first name. His mother, Catherine de l'Estang, spoke Latin and read Greek. She died in 1552, while giving birth to him. Just as soon, the father, struck by emotion, gave his son the rare name of an originary distress: *Agrippa*, that is, *aegre partus*, he who has been born in suffering.

CHAPTER 15

De raptu Pauli

Acts of the Apostles 9:8: Then Saul arose from the earth; and with wide-open eyes, he saw nothingness.

Surrexit Paulus de terra apertisque oculis nihil videbat.

It's Eckhart's most beautiful sermon. About Paul, falling off his horse, discovering that God is nothingness.

Not seeing anything any more, in the excessive brightness, Saul contemplated the vast nothingness of God above him.

What access is there to this world other than bedazzlement, hunger and lack?

The forlorn prince sitting under his tree at noon, on the banks of the Ganges, also says to his disciples:

'There is a proof of the existence of the Void: Lack.'

*

Actually, the apostle *loses* his sight.

'But when Saul arose from the earth, although his eyes were open, he saw nothing'.

It is better to translate humbly 'apertis oculis nihil videbat' by 'his eyes wide open, he saw nothing'. Having

38

been blinded by the too-bright light, the apostle needed to be led by hand by his valets to enter the city of Damascus. He remained for three days without drinking, without seeing, without eating. On the third day, Ananias came and laid his hands upon him.

At this point, the text of the Acts of the Apostles becomes even stranger than the extraordinary reading given to it by Master Eckhart: And immediately *scales* fell from his eyes.

Once the scales had fallen, Saul recovered his sight, and once he had recovered it, he lived in a new name. He discovered a new light in the new name, he ate in his new name, he drank in his new name. He could thus be put, at night, into a basket that was lowered down the ramparts of Damascus so that he could flee without going through the gates of the city.

*

Extraordinary 'scales', in Latin *squamae*, in Greek *lepides*, which cover the apostle's eyes, then fall from his eyelids to the ground.

Triple miracle. He sees the grand light. He doesn't see anything any more. He sees in his new name.

At first, the senses are lost. Following upon the loss of consciousness, new senses are found. With the new senses, a *vita nova* can begin.

At first *Saul* is in total darkness. Then *Paul* suddenly sees.

Saul is a foetus. Paul is born.

Whence the scales. He was a fish.

We were all fish in the former world from which we emerged with an astonishing abruptness.

Every myth explains a current situation by the over-turning of a former situation.

All of a sudden, something unsaddles the soul from the body.

All of a sudden, a love overturns the course of our life.

All of a sudden, an unforeseen death topples the order of the world and especially that of the past, because time is constantly new.

Time is newer and newer and incessantly rushes directly from the origin.

One must once again cross the originary distress as often as one wants to live again.

The trauma of birth, which was the door into this world, is the only door on which one must knock if one wishes to be reborn.

This is how rebirths can take place during the course of life, by reversing this course, by metamorphosing the experience that one had had of it, by leading astray the path that one had taken up to then, by rerouting the journey.

From birth to rebirth, the beginning accumulates.

The experience becomes more and more native.

*

Zhuang Zhou wrote luminously: The life of man between the sky and the earth is like a white horse that leaps over a ravine: a bolt of lightning.

The version of Saint Paul's bedazzlement by the sun at its zenith on the road to Damascus is even simpler: that which unsaddles is time. What de-symbolizes is God.

CHAPTER 16

The Billhook

A billhook is a weapon used to hook onto the bodies of knights to rip them off their saddles and kill them.

CHAPTER 17

Brantôme, Gourville, Montaigne

During the wars of the League, in 1584, Brantôme is unsaddled by a billhook on a lance held by a foot soldier during a battle. Seriously wounded, he is transported to his castle, in Périgord, halfway up a low tower, where he remains bedridden for two years. He was not only thrown from his saddle; he was not only torn away from the war between the Catholics and the Protestants; he was removed from the personal vengeance that he was carrying out.

Vexed, he began to write his memoirs.

In December 1586, when he at last manages to mount a horse again, he gets it galloping just as soon. He joins Catherine de' Medici and Henri de Navarre at the Saint-Brice Château.

Brantôme explains that he has written 'for lack of being able to kill, to love, to ride a horse, to live'.

*

Monsieur de Gourville's Memoirs concerning the affairs for which he has been employed by the Court from 1640 to 1698: I have drafted these Memoirs amid the idleness to which I have found myself reduced by an accident that happened to my right foot after I fell off the saddle of my horse onto the boulders of a hill. The surgeons, after making several incisions in my heel, ordered me to drink vulneraries. I was reduced to such a bad state, towards the end of the year 1696, because of the vulneraries that I had drunk, that I remember having heard a few words during my illness that made me believe that everyone was musing about what they would do after my death. But because my courage was not lacking, I find myself today in the position to hope that my life will be safe this time. I thus begin these memoirs today, 15 June 1702, after having refused the solicitations of several fine-minded people who wanted me to relate the events of my life.

Writing is not living, it is surviving.

Gourville specifies that that writing is a *solicitation* due to an unexpected rebirth and to the desire of the survivors.

Montaigne asserts even more deeply that any writing is an *ecstasy* that time prolongs beyond possible death, once this possibility has been experienced as nearby. This new life is added to the life that has been experienced at its limits. Montaigne then quotes Lucretius: 'No one awakes (*extat*) if he has not felt once the cold of death infiltrating into his veins.'

*

If we cannot aspire to *know* death as long as we live, writes Montaigne in his *Essays* II, 6, then at least we can *try it out*:

In the time of our third or second troubles, going out one day to take a ride for about a league away from my house, thinking myself in all security and so near my retreat that I needed no better equipage, I had taken a horse that trotted easily but was not very strong. Upon my return, one of my men, a big lusty fellow astride a powerful, reckless-mouthed roussin, had got it galloping full speed down my very path, rushing like a colossus upon the little man and the little horse, striking them like a lightning with such strength and weight that it knocked us both over: so that the horse was now lying there, turned over and stunned by the fall, while I was myself ten or twelve paces further on, dead, stretched out face down, my face all battered and broken, my sword, which I had held in my hand, more than ten paces beyond that, and my belt in bits, with no more movement or sentiment in me than a tree stump.

The men surrounding him try to bring Michel de Montaigne back to life.

For two hours, they are unable to do so.

Finally, they raise the rider to his feet.

Once he is up on his feet, Montaigne vomits 'a whole bucketful of pure blood bouillons'.

He comes back to consciousness: I saw the bloody state I was in, my doublet stained all over with the blood that I had vomited. The first thought that came to mind was that I had an arquebus bullet in my head; it's true that several were being fired all around us. It seemed to me that my life was merely hanging on my lips; and I shut my eyes to help push it out, or so it seemed, as I took pleasure in languishing and letting myself go. I believe that this is the same condition in which we see people swooning with weakness in the agony of death; and we pity them without cause. Now that I have indeed tried it out, I have no doubt that until then my judgement had not been right. For, first, being in a swoon, I laboured to rip open the buttons of my doublet with my fingernails. My stomach was so oppressed with the clotting blood that my hands moved all by themselves to that part of the body, as they often do to any itchy spot, against the wishes of our will. Secondly, I ordered that a horse be brought to my wife whom I saw struggling and tiring herself on the road, which is hilly and rugged. However, my condition was, in truth, very mild and peaceful; I had affliction neither for others nor for myself; it was an extreme languor and feebleness, without any pain. I saw my house without recognizing it. When they had put me to bed, I found an inexpressible gentleness in that rest, for I had been desperately tugged and lugged by those poor fellows who had taken pains to carry me on their arms over a long and rough path, and who had by doing so had wearied themselves, twice or thrice one after another. They offered me all sorts of remedies, but I would take none, certain that I was mortally wounded in the head. In truth, it would have been a very happy death, for the weakness of my understanding deprived me of the faculty of discerning, and that of my body of the sense of feeling. I was letting myself slip away so softly and in such a soft and easy manner, that I scarce find any other action less troublesome than that was.

This is how the writing of the *Essays* begins in mortal ecstasy. It is incessantly reproduced, each chapter being a new rebirth, a loss of consciousness followed by a sentiment of pure joy at having survived.

CHAPTER 18

It is no longer a horse. It is a dog. Rousseau is walking down from Ménilmontant. It is the end of the afternoon. He is coming back into Paris, where he plans on dining. Suddenly a ferocious hound emerges, leaps up on him, knocks him over. Rousseau feels neither fear at the size of the dog, nor apprehension at the fierceness of the animal that has surged forth, nor any pain from the blow that has pushed him back and over, for he loses consciousness once he hits the ground.

Night has fallen when he comes back to his senses: I found myself in the arms of three or four young men who told me what had just happened to me.

Jean-Jacques Rousseau is covered with blood but he is incredibly happy.

For Rousseau, it is more than an ecstasy; it is a kind of *contemplation*: The night was growing darker. I perceived the sky, a few stars, and a little vegetation. This first sensation was a delicious moment. I sensed myself only in this way. I was being born, in this instant, to life, and it seemed that I filled all the objects that I perceived with my weightless existence. Completely given over to the present moment, I recalled nothing; I had no distinct notion of my individuality, not the slightest idea of what had just happened to me; I knew neither who I was nor where I was; I felt neither badly, nor fearful, nor worrisome. I watched my blood flowing as I would have watched water flowing in a stream, without imagining that the blood belonged to me in any way. In my entire being, I felt a ravishing calmness to which, every time I that recall it, I find nothing comparable among all the known pleasurable activities.

The depths of the ecstatic soul are without identity.

The depths of autobiography are without autos.

The depths of reading are this same sentiment of self-oblivion. This jubilant self-oblivion. 'I had affliction neither for others nor for myself,' writes Montaigne. 'I knew neither who I was nor where I was,' writes Rousseau.

The dying man experiences no more the moment finishing him off than the conceived human being experiences the origin that has made him.

Although a human being has no possibility of *testing* his end, he is the only example, among all the animals, whose whole life is orientated by the *imagination* of his death.

Although a human being is unable to test his origin, he is the only example, among all the animals, who links pregnancy to sexuality and who prolongs, running counter to himself, upstream from time, the luminous atmospheric life into the dark uterine life where the body had developed. He is the only animal whose life is haunted by the *imagination* of the sexual scene.

A human being is he for whom the invisible conception and the non-anticipatable death are brought together.

This is why, as he recounts Rousseau's fall on the road from Ménilmontant on 24 October 1776, Laurent Jenny writes so admirably: he falls into the origin. He then quotes a page where Buffon (Hist. Nat. VIII, 1749) has Adam say while he is awaking *originarily* to this world: I remember that joyful, unsettling moment when for the first time I sensed my singular existence. I didn't know what I was, where I was, where I had come from. I opened my eyes. What an increase in sensation! The light, the celestial vault, the vegetation on the earth, the crystalline sparkling of the water, everything mattered to me, animated me, and gave me an inexpressible sentiment of pleasure: first and foremost, I believed that all these objects were inside me and were part of me.

*

Every time that one verges on disappearing, that one is stricken with vertigo, lethargy, weakness, or fainting, one must go back through the situation without antecedents, through the initial disorientation within space, through what is unpredictable at the heart of time, through the absence of meaning at the heart of the soul.

Once it is a matter of being *born again*, to be a re-born, a rené, a re-natus, a Renaissant, one must go back through birth, *naissance*.

In no way is death at stake: one must go back through the irruption to redo the irruption.

At stake is the very eruption.

Even if Montaigne, twice, in his extraordinary telling of his horse accident, speaks of the *essay*, of the trial run of death, the experience characteristic of human beings is much more deeply informed by the 'experience-less-ness' of birth.

*

How may one gain access to one's own experience if a human being is he for whom the *periri* is not an *experiri*?

In his *Phenomenology of the Mind*, Hegel wrote: 'In a sacrifice, he who sacrifices identifies with the animal to be sacrificed. He thus dies while he is watching himself. He sees himself as if he were dying, but it is a *comedy*.'

If not a 'comedy', if not a ludibrium, a derision, a mask, a dance, a ceremony, it is an 'imagination' that relies on the spectacle of the death of another person. Every spectacle is based on the two missing scenes (the scene missing for he who is born from it and the scene that is missing for he who has just disappeared into it).

I want to meditate on this strange 'essay', as Montaigne puts it, this trial run of an essay that is without a rough draft, this taste that is without the tasting that could anticipate or prepare it, this entry that is without a noviciate.

I want to think in this book, in this nascent tatter, all bloody with beginnings and rough drafts, this 'experience', this 'experiment' that cannot be repeated even once, this experience beyond all experimentation.

Everyone's life is not an attempt at being. It is the unique attempt, the unique essay, the unique trial run. Our birth is unique, extremely fragile and perilous, semelfactive, making one forsaken, forlorn, infinitely beginning: it is the unique experience.

Life does not know the 'original text' of death. It is unaware of the 'definitive text' into which it pours. But it has at hand the proofs, the printings, the rough drafts, the jottings, the incipits, the manuscripts.

We have 'almost a publication'. We have 'almost an experience'. It is terror, then panic. It is being deafened. It is fainting. It is asphyxia. It is drunkenness when it is carried on too far and the body loses its balance, when the soul loses its memory, when we find ourselves like a child on all fours, on the floor. It is apoplexy. It is being unsaddled. It is dizziness. It is hypnosis. It is coma.

But it is never death: we *miss* the experience.

I suggest distinguishing the missing image of the origin and the missing image of the end.

To the missing originary image is opposed an irresistible imagination that can be evoked by using the German noun Urszene.

To the missing mortal image is opposed an irresistible imagination that can be evoked by using the Greek noun Nekuia.

Like the Urszene, the Nekuia is a universal datum.

The theme of going through death or across the world of the dead by the hero, the sovereign, the god, or the creator is attested in numerous myths, tales, legends, stories.

Gilgamesh goes down into the Underworld, as does the Japanese god Izanagi, Orpheus, Ulysses, Jesus, Dante, and so on.

The experience of the Nekuia is this: 'He is both dead and still alive.'

CHAPTER 19

The Marshal of La Palisse's Horse

A line of verse is modified by means of a single letter at the end of a sad song. La Palisse was the eldest son of Geoffroy de Chabannes. His mother was the maid of honour for Queen Marie. His face expressed such mildness and beauty that he was loved, during his childhood, by the son of King Louis XI. He was a counsellor, then the King's favourite, then the chamberlain, then the General Captain. One day the French left to re-conquer the kingdom of Naples. They took the Alpine route. They reached Italy. The Marshal of La Palisse was the commander of everyone. One fine morning, as the haze was lifting, they spotted a troop of horsemen. The marshal wanted to give chase to them. But while pursuing them, the marshal and his men rode down into the depths of a valley and found themselves caught in fog. It was 25 February 1525. It was eight in the morning. It happened that the fog thickened more than it scattered as the sun rose. Its thickness had so increased by nine o'clock that it formed a kind of snow. La Palisse managed to muster his troops, but when he wanted to leave the valley his horse was killed beneath him. He was thrown backwards from the saddle; a squire going by the name of Nicolas de Saint Pal had to intervene to help him get back up with his heavy suit of armour; but La Palisse's thigh had been run through; he couldn't remain standing; another horse had to be found in a hurry; Pierre de Buisson shouted that he was going to give him his own; he headed towards him but arrived too late. The Italian Lord Castaldo had already made him prisoner. It happened that Buzarto, the infantry captain, seeing that the prisoner was the Marshal of France, demanded to have the right of capture, which Castaldo refused. Buzarto then aimed his arquebus, shooting it at point-blank range into the breastplate of the Marshal of La Palisse, who died immediately, thrown backwards into the mud by the force of the arquebus shot.

*

With La Palisse dead, his troops disperse into the fog.

The enemy similarly scatters into the haze.

The Duke of Alençon and his troops flee.

King François I is fighting a battle at Mirabello. When the loss of the Marshal of France is announced to him, he simply says:

'It's a misadventure.'

Bonnivel, whose flank has been run through by three thrusts of a lance, falls dead over the neck of his horse, which gallops off who knows where with him.

Similarly, the great squire Gallias de Saint Séverin dies yet remains in the saddle and rides, dead, through the battle.

The horse of the King of France also finally falls. François I, hampered when he walks because of the long pointed poulaines on his feet, hides in a beetroot silo. It is eleven in the morning. He is discovered among the beetroots. He is taken prisoner. He takes off his cursed poulaines. Half-naked, he is escorted to the Cascina Repentita.

*

The Duke of Bourbon signed a peace settlement and received from Castaldo's hands the body of the Marshal of France. He had it transported into Saint Augustine's Church in Pavia. Woodworkers prepared a coffin. Two physicians treated the body with 'myrrh and aloes'. Then the soldiers transported the coffin to the Church of Treignat. On 19 March, the embalmed body of the Marshal of La Palisse was given its funeral, presided over by the Duke of Bourbon, who had donned mourning clothes. Then the men of his house desired to chant their plaints over the body of their master while taking it to its grave. The Duke of Bourbon granted their request. He asked the Marshal's secretary, whose name was Jean de Paris, to draft them. The funeral procession, accompanied by soldiers, took the mountain road. The journey was made in the greatest sorrow, the troop chanting every hour the plaints written down by Jean de Paris. The plaints began with these words:

'Alas, La Palisse is dead!

Near Pavia he died.

Alas, if he weren't dead,

Envious others would be.'

Weariness, malice, chance, air, the Alps blended into their chanting.

Small letters turned.

'Envious others would be' became 'alive he'd still be'.

On 3 April, the procession arrived in Lyons, where a new funeral was celebrated in Saint John's Cathedral. The cortège re-formed, the procession departed, the chanting began once again, and the final obsequies were held in Lapalisse on 9 April 1525 in the presence of the horse of honour of the Marshal of La Palisse, all alone, at the head of the cortège, covered with a black cloth dragging on the ground.

The horse of honour was followed by the helmet and the sword, the black baton and spurs.

Then came his eldest son, etc.

Everyone was chanting:

Alas if he were not dead

Alive he'd still be.

CHAPTER 20

A horse, a horn, a sword, a pine tree. It is spring 778. It is the beginning of the history of France.

Our history begins with an unsaddled rider who brandishes a sword that doesn't break.

With a horn that calls out in vain.

Count Roland, having put the olifant to his mouth, sounds it three times. Sounds it louder and louder. In vain. The knight has blown with such force that his mouth is full of blood.

CHAPTER 21

The Beach at Carnac

The Carnac alignments are lists of the dead sinking into the sea. Migrating birds gather on the same sites when they are leaving, which is also a song. As they suddenly fly off all together, they seem to obey a single orientation which, for them, is fully evident. The birds are souls which, as they assemble at the end of the earth, all of a sudden take flight for their country located at the end of the sky. For all souls leave for nourishment in the West of the bloody sky. In Carnac, the dining room of the Hôtel des Bains looked out on the salt beds. Every morning we walked on the gorse-lined path along the beach before crossing the meadows. Small, completely white herons, with a foot in the air, in the sunlight, which I see once again, so distinctly, in the depths of my skull, as I write. They wade prudently through the whitish sludge, raising each leg above the water before plunging it down again, beyond their strange knee.

Arriving at the Pointe des Calaros, there are two black parasol pines, near the roar of the sea, which are the most beautiful in the world. They are more beautiful than the pines of Eden. We walk through the village of Saint-Colomban, always deserted in winter. We walk faster. They are not dead people; they are worse than dead people; they are rich people; they are 'absent occupants' who have paid a lot of money for their closed doors, their rolled-down shutters, their sirens ready to screech at the slightest fly moving by, at the slightest thread coming out of a spider at the moment when it is building its web by gradually swinging in front of the alarm placed in an angle of the wall.

*

Orientation derives from the eyesight of the predators. It consists of making the eyes converge; it consists of using muscles to bring two visions towards a single target of hunger or desire.

Then binocular vision, dragging along the rest of the body with it, itself becomes haste, leaping, snatching, fusion.

Now it's reading.

Eyesight having become at once localization of the prey and the shooting distance.

The body having become a muscular bit of time that crouches to be able to spring suddenly, in anticipation of the mortal capture.

In animals that move forward by focusing their two eyes on the object whose lack they feel ever-more violently, the localization and the locomotion seem separated in time: in fact, this separation between the prey and the predator *invents* time.

The desiring time is this rending between prey and predator, even as time become language is the narrative of predation returning from the death that has been given.

Predation and narration are from the same origin. Even among bees. Worker bees, the 'rapporteuses' who bring back pollen, are also predators and tattlers. There is already a 'sous-venir' (memory) 'beneath' them when they come back buzzing.

So it is with language. Because localization temporally precedes locomotion, this bringing back, this 're-porting', this 'tattling' (rapportage), hollows out the orientation in space. The orient is always that which has been lost and which one lacks all the more because it makes one starve. The distension of time is a rending between the orient of the place and the movement within the place (between being on the look-out and the capture). The orientation is a temporal rhythm in which the time of displacement is scheduled during the time of the pause. The wandering of the hunter, once the prey is found and is dead, has become travelling. Travelling means travel writing. The bees tell of their travelling: this is how flowers have found the means to address themselves, by dancing, to the queen who has remained in the shadows and who doesn't see them.

CHAPTER 22

Quo itis?

'Where are you coming from? Where are you going?' the innkeeper asked him.

The Roman knight did not respond.

With his hand, the innkeeper invited the knight to sit.

The Roman knight did not sit.

The innkeeper spoke again:

'I thank you for coming into my inn because I feel more and more lonely here. I am at the end of the world. Here, company is rare. Excuse me if I wish to speak to you.'

The Roman knight accepted the bowl of warm wine that the innkeeper held out to him, but he didn't say a word and remained standing. The innkeeper continued:

'I was feeling bored when I heard your horse's hooves on the pebbles. Now your horse is chewing its hay and here you are, drinking a bowl of warm wine in front of me. Look at this crackling fire. I think that you should take off your raincoat and sit down within the hearth. Your tunic and your short Gallic coat will dry out more quickly. Put your butt down on that seat in the hearth, which should be very warm. You will feel well there.'

The knight did not take off his coat. He did not enter the hearth. He did not answer his host.

He set down the burning bowl on the brick, knelt in front of the hearth, reached out his hands.

The flames licked his hands, which had become white and almost translucent.

After a little while, the innkeeper again asked the knight:

'At least may I ask you: where are you going?'

But the Roman knight did not answer. He stood back up. Standing beneath the stone mantle of the hearth, he rubbed with his two palms the coarse flesh and hairs of his thighs to warm them.

Then he bent down and picked up his bowl, which he had left on the white brick. He began to drink again, while blowing on the surface of the wine. He drank all the wine. He closed his eyelids.

Time went by.

Much later, opening his eyes and staring at the fire, the knight murmured, without looking at the innkeeper:

'A while ago, you asked me where I was going.'

'Yes'.

'I was cold.'

'Yes.'

'I was very cold.'

'Yes.'

'I didn't answer because I didn't know what to answer.'

'Yes.'

The Roman knight was speaking very softly. His voice was muffled. He did not need to look at the person to whom he was speaking. He asked:

'Now it's my turn to ask you a question.'

'If you wish', said the innkeeper.

'Do you believe that because one spends a lifetime sitting on the saddle of a horse, one is going somewhere?'

The innkeeper did not reply.

'Well?' the knight asked, turning to the innkeeper.

'Nothing', answered the innkeeper.

Then the knight added:

'I don't know exactly where I am going, but I am going to tell you what I think about this journey that I undertook thirteen years ago. I have an appointment with death. I don't know where this appointment has been set up. Birds migrate over extremely long distances when they are pressured by the cold. Sometimes men act like birds in winter. Birds like fog to close in around them in the sky. Horses like fog to close in around them when they gallop over the infinite steppe. Ships like fog to close in around them when they sail off over the sea at daybreak. Men like fog to close in around them in the form of language.'

Chest, croup, mane, penis—everything in a horse is more beautiful, more voluminous, faster, more superb than a man's torso, than a man's buttocks, than the hair that grows on the skull of a man, than a man's penis.

The horse is perhaps the only animal that man has uncontestably found to be more handsome than himself.

The word 'cauchemar' (nightmare) refers to a mare that weighs down on the breasts of dreaming women. This immense body sitting on the self oppresses dreadfully.

An immense noise of galloping in the sky: it's a storm. I evoke the black, impenetrable cloud that assaults, coming from the depths of the celestial vault and devouring the site.

It's Hennequin's madness.

It's the magic horse-ride.

Rain falling suddenly in gusts produces an infernal noise and makes the ground tremble. Do peasants see time going by? At least they never see the face of the rider mounting it. They hear the immense horse passing by above them. They see the rain rebounding luminously like lines on walls, stones, cobblestones, roof tiles, slate tiles, the leaves of trees, the water of ponds, pools, lakes, seas.

*

In sexuality, one 'recognizes' immediately what one was 'unaware of' until then, but one does not 'look at' it for all that.

The genital organ desires the other genital organ that it discovers, without examining it. The eye does not contemplate the spot where the body seeks its pleasure. In sexuality, time is outstripped and the genitals are *concealed* inside the embrace. Desire outstrips the entire sexual scene in which it participates. Finally, desire curtly tosses the soul into disappointment, the body into dis-excitement, both into a stark vision of the abyss and the distress of the first day, when nothing had really been perceived.

*

Time is that which devours everything, including itself. That which snaps up everything and which, at high speed, flees from itself. Time is as irretrievable as the javelin that the hunter has just thrown by letting go of it into the air element. Time cannot be called back into Being. It is like the irretrievable course of Zhuang Zhou's horse in space. Horses imagine death because they transport men with matchless speed.

Rapidus, rapax, raptus are the same word.

Horses are 'raptors' par excellence.

A horse which is going to flee abruptly, but which first rears up, immense, neighing, standing on its hind legs, is the

Ur-animal. The originary loss, the abrupt flight, the departure with no return, the abrupt move: this is the genealogy of time long before death, long before the bloody body consumed by a dead, immobile God.

CHAPTER 24

One day, Abraham asked Oesterer:

'What is faster than a man on a horse?'

But Oesterer was busy saying the rosary. He didn't raise his eyes. He was murmuring his prayers. (He believed neither in God nor in the Devil but he incessantly whispered prayers.)

'Memory,' murmured Meaume, who was engraving a copper plate on the table, surrounded by a fruit dish, a book, a Venetian mirror, and three candles.

His upper lip was trembling and he stopped speaking, exhausted after uttering this single word, memory. The engraver only rarely opened his mouth. Speaking made his heart beat fast.

Abraham turned towards Meaume the Engraver. He saw the hideous head of the painter bent over the three flames.

'Why are you weeping, Monsieur Meaume?' Abraham asked softly.

But Meaume let his tears flow.

One evening, the engraver confided to Esther, who was sitting beside him at the table where he etched—surrounded by his candles, his fruit dish, his mirror, his magnifying glass and his burnisher—that he often saw at night, in a dream, the face of a young woman whom he had once known in Bruges. The dream could awake him in the middle of the night. He would find his lower abdomen all excited, in the heart of night, his face covered with sweat, because of the unforeseeable image comprised in the dream.

These faces coming back from beyond time, beyond place, beyond the lives of the living, beyond the deaths of the dead, did not give him joy alone.

Sometimes there were real fears, real staggering panic-ridden fears produced by these reappearing faces.

He sometimes drew what he had perceived in this world of memories, to drag it outside of him and with the willingness to distance himself from it. To get rid of it by setting it down on a piece of paper. To sometimes burn this piece of paper straight out. To remove it from his days.

'It's true that the images are frightening at first. It's true what you say,' Esther confided to him. 'As for myself, I often see my father's face as if he were there. He's shouting his head off at me. So I also start shouting with all my force to make him run off. I wake up with my genitals all relaxed and wet. My breasts are excited and covered with water. My buttocks are also full of water. However, my father has been dead for a long time. Nonetheless, I am wet as if I were being born into this world. The faces of our ancestors catch us unawares by leaping out of nothingness and out of time. Their features seem brand new. These images cover us with water, with piss, with shouting, but, at bottom, it's marvellous. It's pure desire that sees them.'

CHAPTER 25

De raptu charu

Why does the god of death, for the ancient Etruscans, carry a small hammer in his hand? Because this hammer was called a *korax* in the Etruscan language. And the word *korax* means crow in the Greek language. This is why the god of death has the hooked nose of the eagle, as does the head of the hammer itself at the moment when one wants to strike.

As for his ears, they were drawn like the perked ears of deers. They were extremely attentive, pointed, erectile, erected, savage, mobile, perked ears.

His beard is growing old. His tousled hair looks like many snakes rising up and swaying to the passing breeze.

A short tunic barely conceals his penis, which is like a small green viper.

His skin is dark blue.

This bird of prey to which are added a wild animal and a dragon is nicknamed the Ravisher in Etruscan.

Pain makes him laugh, revealing his sharp yellow teeth.

One quickly has a liking for smiles, one irresistibly borrows them from the lips of one's mother, one likes to reproduce them on the lips of she whom one loves, one loves to place them on younger lips. An atrocious seductiveness is passed on in an almost involuntary, almost animalistic way, seeking prematurely to stop all violence by means of submission, retracted claws, squinting eyes, clenched fangs.

A smile is that which keeps the mouth closed.

A laugh is that which opens the jaws. Then it entirely clears the way for the teeth and so begins the capture and death.

*

On the volumen that he holds in his left hand, the Etruscan god of death, Charu, inscribes not only the name of the corpse but also his titles of kinship.

In his right hand, he carries his hammer with which he begins tapping three times on the skull of the dead man or woman; then he batters it; he opens the skull; he eats the brains before preserving the head, which is henceforth imputrescible. Now this is why the Etruscan korax precedes the Roman imago. Thot, the god of lightning, at least in northern Europe, also holds in his hand a hammer, but that does not have the same signification as Charu's hammer. The hammer blows are thunderbolts from the divine black-smith. He drives nails into the sky in the form of stars that establish destinies.

*

The god's hammer strikes down human beings even as the sacrificer's mallet strikes down animals at the moment of sacrifice.

The sacrifice defines the flesh-eating revelries filched from predators.

Every soothsayer is a flesh-eater.

Thus all the gods give consent to only bloody sacrifices and mobilize all the wars between nations.

*

In General History, it happens that no society has offered to its gods a feast of mosquitoes or white fish, of viruses, crayfish, squids, white cuttlefish, or snails.

A sacrifice with red meat is the human ritual even as the making of honey is the ritual of bees.

If hunting is the murder of an animal in order to eat it, then religion is the murder of a man in the same way that he was killed by a wild animal—that is, the old god—in days of old.

Every temple is a slaughterhouse. Every altar is a cutting stone. Every silence is an impatient, guilty hunger.

Abrupt excitement full of dread set off by the sudden over-exciting scream, which brings the group members together, which creates the union and the exaltation of everyone by means of the common meal, the mouths opening and chewing bloodily even as the mouth is opened in human language, the group once again divided up according to the spurting blood, the group hierarchized through the attribution of the parts that are marvellous because they are completely red.

CHAPTER 26

Mettius Curtius' Horse

There was one horse, in human history, which was frightened by the human noise of war.

It preferred dying to serving men in war.

This is the Roman legend of Mettius Curtius' horse.

It is especially the origin of Curtius Lake.

Mettius Curtius died in the swamps where his horse had thrown him while killing itself.

Nothing is more touching than the appearance of this lake where a horse wanted to leave the human shore. However, everything is sad there. The foam on the shore, in the middle of summer, is red like an autumn fern. The water moving along the shore is more naked and heavy than everywhere else. The wake that follows the plastic hull of the dinghy struggles to rise. Silence itself is strange there, as if the air were weighing down, on the sad lake, with an infinite heaviness. The mayflies keep swarming four centimetres above the surface of the water, as offerings to the wide-open jaws of thousands of motionless fish that watch more than devour them.

*

It's this same Mettius Curtius who declared to Tullius, at the origins of Rome:

'The choice is not to be free or a slave. The choice is between master and slave.'

This is pure Freud. This is harsh Marx. One attributes King Servius Tullius the invention of social classes (the invention of classicism). First, two classes opposed each other: prima classis and secunda classis. Such was Roman violence.

Predator / prey.

In Rome, dominus / servus.

Later, eternity / the century.

CHAPTER 27

A Gloomy Story

A blacksmith-farrier lived in the village of Toucy in the old duchy of Burgundy. He was very poor. He shoed horses in a wooden stocks so worm-eaten that it collapsed on him one day while he was forging. The blacksmith was so poor that he had no means to set it back upright. His name was Larousse. He had a son whose name was Pierre.

Pierre became even poorer than his father. So poor that he was forced, in 1849, to sell the notecards that he filled with notes about the books that he had read.

CHAPTER 28

Freud in Cologne

Freud had four dogs: Lün (1), Jofie, Lün (2), Jumbo.

*

Freud was born in a blacksmith's house. Even more specifically, in a first-floor flat rented out by a wool merchant to a blacksmith-farrier, above the chimney of a forge, a wooden horseshoeing stocks, a henhouse and a slurry puddle. He cries out for the first time there on 6 May 1856. He is circumcised on the 13th. Escape to Breslau. Escape to Leipzig. Finally, the Vienna ghetto, Mazzesinsel, in the second district, near the Prater and its avenues lined with horse chestnut trees.

On 1 May 1873, Empress Sisi and Emperor Franz-Joseph inaugurate the World's Fair while Freud, who is preparing his baccalaureate exams, gazes on with marvel.

*

In August 1908, Freud goes alone on holiday, alone on a trip. He goes to England. He wants to see his two brothers again, Emanuel and Philipp, who emigrated there in 1859.

When he arrives in Cologne, he gets lost in the city. Near the train station, he raises his eyes and is impressed by the beauty of the cathedral. He hesitates to push the immense door. He doesn't dare to push it. He goes back to the station, but he has not escaped fast enough from the place that has caused his anxiety. The memory of those who have died, of those who have fled, of the deaths in his own family, flood back over him. His memory immediately becomes vaster. It heads further back into the warmth of the end of day. It is another month of August that surges forth: the month of August 1349. The crowd of Christians invades the Jewish quarter, sets fire to houses, the Mikvel, the synagogue, the old people's home, the library, the cemetery. In a single night, the most important Jewish community of Germany is annihilated. Why does Freud like Jensen so much? It is not only because of *Gradiva*. It is because of another of Jensen's novels, titled *The Jews of Cologne*, which enjoyed much success in 1869. Freud writes: I examined the train schedule. My hesitations had made me miss my connection. I first wondered if I shouldn't stay overnight in Cologne. This resolution was inspired in me by a pious sentiment because, according to a family tradition, my ancestors had once fled from this city to escape persecutions. But I changed my mind. I told myself that I needed to flee exactly as they had done. I decided to leave by another train for Rotterdam, where I arrived in the middle of the night. I took advantage of the detour to see Rembrandt's magnificent paintings in The Hague.

CHAPTER 29

The Horseshoeing Stocks

During the First World War, my grandfather kept his personal diary in Latin, in his trench, wearing his helmet, sitting near his bayonet, his little eyes behind his grey, round-rimmed, steel glasses.

He was from Givet.

We would spend our holidays a few kilometres from Givet, in Chooz, the village from which our family stemmed, until an atomic power station devastated the hamlet and turned it into a town before making a future bomb out of it.

*

In Rome, the horseshoeing stocks, the tri-palium, was 'the three-post tool' that enabled one to attach a horse to shoe it or a slave to punish him. Then this tool of the slave's torment comes to mean any laborious activity that is both oppressive and unpleasant.

The blacksmith-farrier of the small village of Chooz was nicknamed Père Français. Père Français had received his nickname from his twin brother, who had settled just on the other side of the forest, that is, on the other side of the border, that is, on the other side of the Meuse, and who was called Père Belge.

Each brother, in his country, served as a blacksmith-farrier, even as each brother had received his nickname from the other brother.

In Chooz, all this was at once a big wooden horseshoeing stocks standing on the cobblestones of the street, a forge, a tobacco shop, a stamp shop.

As long as I was a toddler and didn't know how to read—then as long as I didn't have the whimsical notion of withdrawing into my reading (at the age of five) and of losing my identity in it during a journey nourishing in turn an endless travel story—I would sit on the gutter stones of the main street and watch Père Français slowly burning the hoof horn while the gigantic animal was shaking his head and whinnying.

I liked the intense stench and the fright incited in me by the immense workhorses from the surrounding farms as well as the two big white horses of my cousin the beer brewer.

I liked the Ardennes draught horses, which were enormous, robust, placid. I liked to admire their foals in the pastures and reedy marshlands along the Meuse. I liked the nags that languidly harrowed the ploughed fields, that slowly returned, right in the middle of the road, harnessed to small carts, to long hay wagons, to wagons with tyres, without worrying about cars, horns, shouts, and peacefully going back to my family's farms that stood along the border line from Chooz to Givet, Nichet, Feschaux, and the Aubrives Quarries.

All day long, Père Français vigorously tapped the rivets on the horseshoes that had emerged fuming and bright white from the fire, and that he held by means of a long black pair of pincers.

*

I stayed for hours, for hours, for hours, squatting in front of the big wooden horseshoeing stocks, my hands on my naked knees. All work for me is, first of all, this wooden structure into which a jibbing horse is inserted.

Père Français also forged irons, billhooks, scythes, harnesses, ploughshares, little bells.

He repaired locks.

He also managed to get the job done as far as rifles were concerned.

*

Now old, when all that is no more and when this 'more' diminishes until it becomes no more than a line, I am still squatting in front of the blacksmith. I hear the extraordinarily sharp, gleaming tap of the hammer on the anvil. I hear the cry of the whinnying horses inside the horseshoeing stocks, kicking their big legs amid the stench of the burnt live flesh. I remember or perhaps imagine that the ring used by the blacksmith-farrier to make the horse back up inside the stocks was called a tord-nez (nose-twister). I see the thick, almost entirely black leather apron on which the hoof was placed. I see the hoof stand, also made of leather. The blacksmith-farrier would firmly place the hoof on this leather stand. He would begin by trimming, by hallowing out, by rasping; then he would prepare the horseshoe; then he would round it out on the anvil until it had the exact shape of the hoof. He would heat it until it became red. He would place it on the horse's hoof 'just to see': this was called the *essai* (trial run). All the hoof horn would start fuming; then he would put the horseshoe back into the fire; he would re-sculpt it on the anvil; he would plunge it into the water; more fuming; he would finally come back towards the horse. He was always working. When there was no horse in the stocks, when he wasn't selling lumpy Scaferlati tobacco, yellow or pale-green stamps, packages of Gauloises blue cigarettes for my uncles, he would repair the farmers' wheelbarrow wheels, my brewer-cousins' hand-truck wheels, my brothers' bicycle wheels.

CHAPTER 30

Horsehair

The tale of Damoklès shows him lying on the golden bed of Dionysius of Syracuse, the Tyrant. He is eating succulent foods, like everything that can be found in Syracuse. The slaves and servants around him are naked and anticipate all his desires, turning them immediately into delectations at the very instant he imagines them. The sword suspended by Dionysius just above Damoklès' head hangs from a *strand of horsehair*.

*

Caravaggio, when he came to Sicily, asked Vincenzo Mirabella to take him to visit Dionysius' prisons. When they arrive at the Latomie Quarry, they dismount from their horses, toss down a rope, go down to the bottom of the abyss. It's Caravaggio himself who, in 1608, gave the name of 'Dionysius' Ear' to the sonorous grotto in which every-thing can be heard, the cave in which Dionysius kept Plato prisoner.

*

One day, Socrates' demon said to him: 'Be a horsefly on the back of a horse.' Afterwards, Socrates absurdly translated these profound words uttered by his demon. He thought that they meant: 'Become a philosopher in the streets of the city. In shop after shop, sting the brains of your fellow citizens. Die for the fame of the town.' Yet his demon had contented itself with telling him: 'Be a horsefly on the back of a horse.'

*

Nicholas of Cusa wrote in *De sapientia II*: Men, we should call you horses. Each of you is like a horse (*quasi equus*) which, free by nature, has let himself be bound by the tamer with a muzzle (*capistro alligatus*) to the wooden feeding trough from which the horse eats nothing but what has been brought there.

Your intellect,

being tied to the authority of other men who have written and whom you read,

eats foreign nourishment (*pabulo alieno*)

and not the hay ripening on the hillside,

not the water flowing down and following the very shape of the field it irrigates,

not the daylight shining on it,

not the night that moistens it with its dew and nourishes it, all of which are much more incomprehensible than books,

even if they are nothing more than the incomprehensible interruption of the language spoken by men in Being.

For there where the seasons unfurl,

where valleys and heaths extend,

where seas go forward,

where mountains rise beneath the sky,

tell me, one day, why did shouts and songs appear?

CHAPTER 31

Apelles

One day Apelles gave up when he was painting the head of a horse. He threw the sponge against the wall. Suddenly (exaiphnès) he painted it.

Sextus wrote: In the same sudden manner, non-trouble follows as if by chance the renunciation to judgement, without the connection being visible.

Freud: In the same way, suddenly loved, the symptom falls one fine day.

In the same way, at the Saint-Antoine Hospital, one February day, vomiting blood, throwing in the sponge, I found the form of this last realm where I now live, striding over time, sitting with my feet in the gutter, examining old work collapsing where a horse is weeping.

*

Man must go back to the unforeseeable as his country.

The unforeseeable, nothing else.

The unforeseeable means time, darkness, the spurt of sperm, the originary site, the earth, the sunlight, the unpredictable beauty of nature, the exploding depths of the sky.

The Without-Essay.

Indeed, the Unforeseeables (more than the Fundamentals) form the subject matter of his quest and of his hunger.

They are the Angels.

Horses that speed off, tigers that spring,

dolphins that fly up over the sparkling surface of the sea,

sharks that snap,

vultures that fly down all of a sudden from the heights of the sky,

lightning, loves, waves, cyclones,

spring piercing through the snow,

such is the unforeseeable 'inhuman' (at least the ante-human unpredictability of life in nature, of nature in matter, of matter flying through the void of the sky).

Lightning bolts that unexpectedly strike oaks, which they set on fire, even as children fall when they are born, while crying, while singing to breathe all of a sudden.

CHAPTER 32

Phaethon

Phaethon was driving the sun's horses.

In the middle of the sky, suddenly frightened by the wild animals outlined by the motionless stars, the child lets go of the reins. The chariot he was driving tips over.

He falls.

But his body doesn't crash on the earth: his father, balancing the lightning bolt near his right ear (dextra libratum fulmen ab aure), strikes down his son with lightning *before he reaches the ground*.

*

He is senseless *before he dies*.

Spinoza wrote in *Ethica* II, 18: Miles visis in arena equi vestigiis statim ex cogitatione equi in cogitationem equitis et inde in cogitationem belli etc. incident. At rusticus equi, aratri, agri etc.

I like Spinoza's etc.'s, which evoke infinity.

(A soldier seeing horse tracks in the sand will immediately move from the thought of a horse to the thought of a horseman and from there to the thought of war, etc. On the contrary, a peasant seeing horse tracks in the sand will immediately think of the plough, the furrow, sowing, harvest, etc.)

CHAPTER 33

Nietzsche's Horse in 1621, 1877, 1889

Nietzsche wrote: 'A horse carries you, such are metaphors.' After the *transfers* that transform non-speakers who shout loudly into figureheads who speak incessantly, *metaphors* mean *horses* that are going to run at full speed within language, bounding from stone to stone, from face to face, from word to word, from text to text, from image to image, as in dreams.

*

It was the eye of the horse ridden by Antonio Giulio Brignole that distressed Nietzsche in Genoa. He immediately jotted it down in his notebook, in 1877, as he was leaving the Palazzo Rosso.

Van Dyck painted this eye in 1621.

Nietzsche simply notes that Van Dyck's horse eye is 'full of pride' and that seeing it had suddenly 'got him back on his feet' whereas he had been completely depressed.

Eleven years later, in April 1888, Nietzsche rents a room at 6 *via* Carlo Alberto in Turin. When he goes out, he crosses the square, takes the side path, follows the bank of the Po River.

On 3 January 1889, on the Piazza Carlo Alberto, in front of the fountain, he watches an old humiliated horse beaten violently by its owner. The horse looks at Nietzsche with such pain that he runs over to it, hugs it and loses his mind forever.

*

What does 'hug a humiliated horse' mean? It means: to bemoan domestication.

Simonides wrote in his praise of Sparta: The citizens are horses (hippoi) that are tamed into herds (agelai). This is why the city (polis) should be called The Man-Tamer.

*

One day, Nietzsche summed up what he meant by the over-turning of Western values: the so-called aristocratic Greek values (what is strong is beautiful, what is noble is good, Dionysus rips apart and eats raw meat, whoever is lucky is loved by the gods) are gradually opposed, in the Empire of the Romans, by Jewish and Christian values (whoever is weak is emotionally moving, whoever is poor is good, God preferred the slave's cross, one who suffers goes to paradise).

In fact, this thesis of a 'reversal' or 'overturning' occurs much earlier than Christianity.

The inversion does not even disguise the originary relation because it *reproduces* it. Language is this reflection. Language opposes *just as soon*.

As soon *said*, there is inversion.

What is worthwhile for you is worthwhile for me (he who waters is watered, the biter is bit, the predator is devoured).

*

The inversion already belongs to animal thought. All predators are afraid of becoming prey. Dreams stage all the situations, in any direction.

*

Pauson is the first poor painter—that is, an irrepressible painter and a poor painter—in the history of painting.

Aristophanes said of him: 'He preferred fasting to not painting.' (The sentence can be inversed: He painted so much he fasted.)

Pauson was especially well known because of his painting titled *Horse Rolling in Dust*.

The work was executed with unbelievable realism.

But Lucian wrote that Pauson had simply *turned the painting upside down*.

As for Plutarch, he wrote in De Pyth. V: Pausôn katestrepse ton pinaka. That is, Pauson catastrophed (overturned) the painting.

Of course, this anecdote about the painting turned upside down or overturned against the wall of the painter's studio is legendary. The story runs through the history of painting. It can be found again, told in an almost identical way, in the biographies of Kandinsky, Giacomo Balla, Klee, Mondrian, Malevitch.

*

The predatory tension is always uncertain. The viewpoint of the predator and the viewpoint of the prey turn, are exchanged, are overturned endlessly. No one knows, when forehead meets forehead, body meets body, antler meets antler, rack meets rack, face meets face, jaw meets jaw, who will eat, who will be eaten.

Who will be fascinating, who will be fascinated.

Who will be the thesis, who will be the antithesis.

Who will spring and devour, who will remain pinned to the ground and be gulped down.

This tragic aporia, this *carnivalesque* anguish, is not specific to humanity. It is not even specific to flesh-eaters. This background is ante-human.

Watch the stag watching, suddenly motionless, at the top of a hill, when its ears turn towards a mysterious sound, when its eyes become misty with fear or distress.

CHAPTER 34

Gunnar Unsaddled

Gunnar said farewell to his family and hopped up on the saddle. He jog-trotted up to the boat that was going to keep him from being hunted down by the Icelandic barons and take him all the way to Norway. All of a sudden, his horse stumbled; Gunnar falls to the ground.

He finds himself sitting in oats; he looks around; he sees the hill; he gazes at the slopes covered with crops; in the distance, he spots the farm that he built.

He gets up. All of a sudden, as he is standing motionless in the countryside, he slowly turns around; the sky is pure.

In the distance, he sees the ocean.

On the other side of the fjord, he notices the volcano.

He says:

'I prefer to die earlier. Never mind if I die earlier. I want to remain within this beauty.'

Nietzsche always arrived from the lake. Once his rowboat drew alongside the shore, he grasped the innkeeper's hand and found himself on the grey wooden pontoon just in front of the hotel. There were two larches standing there, near the cabin. He lived alone in Sils-Maria. He wrote. His sister Elisabeth (Fritz called her Lieschen) had accompanied her husband to South America. In Paraguay, Bernard Förster and Lieschen had founded a German ecological colony devoted to the 'regeneration of humanity'. An institution with a promising future to which they had given the name 'Germania'. Friedrich Nietzsche, who had remained alone in Sils-Maria, in the Swiss canton of Grisons, drafted *On the Genealogy of Morals*. Then he took the road once again for Nice. Finally, he arrived in Venice. *The Case of Wagner* appeared in Germany and met with great success. Then he settled in Turin. The last letter that he received from his sister was written on 6 September 1888 and sent from Paraguay; it arrived exactly on 15 October 1888, for his birthday. Beginning in November, Nietzsche is happy. Little by little, his success, blending with his joy, makes him delirious. At the end of the year, he sends to all his friends the 'letters of madness'. On 9 January 1889, Overbeck comes to fetch him and takes him, from Turin, back to Basel where he entrusts the ecstatic philology professor to his mother's safekeeping. In 1897, when their mother dies, Elisabeth Nietzsche-Förster alone takes care of her brother; she decides to move, the two of them settling in Weimar, where he dies in 1900, after Freud had published *The Interpretation of Dreams* nine months earlier, in Vienna and Leipzig.

CHAPTER 36

Sejus' Horse

It happened that the horse belonging to Sejus brought ill fortune to everyone who had ridden it.

Cneius Sejus, Dolabella, Cassius, Mark Anthony—everyone who had ridden it died.

In France, the old chroniclers who wrote during the reigns of Charles IX, Henri III, Henri IV and Louis XIII, said of Marguerite de Valois that she was a 'Sejus' horse'. All her lovers died a violent death on the day following their lovemaking with her.

Martigue's throat was slit. La Mole was beheaded. Bussy d'Amboise was murdered.

This is why the Romans, at the onset of the Empire, gave the name of 'Sejus' horse' to what nineteenth-century Americans would call a 'femme fatale'.

*

It has even been written of Louise de Vitry that she was a 'Sejus' horse'. However, the successive deaths of her lovers were far from being as immediate as those following lovemaking with Marguerie de Valois. But the Duke of Guise, Charles d'Humières, and the Count of Randau, after they had much loved her, felt ill, then got worse, then breathed their last breath.

At the end of her life, thinking back on her life, Louise de Vitry abruptly sat up motionlessly in her bed, suddenly worried.

It seemed that she had perked up her ears in the surrounding air, attentive to a kind of song. She brutally turned her face to the right, looked for a moment at the prelate who had confessed her, and asked him:

'Is love a mortal sin?'

The Cardinal du Perron replied:

'No. You would be dead.'

CHAPTER 37

Comploter

Chalais was executed on 19 August with thirty-seven axe blows.

Once Chalais was dead, the Duchess of Chevreuse gave herself to La Rochefoucauld.

Who is the Duke of La Rochefoucauld? The greatest French writer.

Who is the greatest French writer? A man who was a direct descendant of Melusine the Fairy.

*

Comploter (Let's Plot) was the nickname used by Jacques Esprit, the Court and the Academy to refer to the Duchess of Chevreuse.

All of a sudden, in his coach rushing through the night, La Rochefoucauld asked, with his soul swiftly aroused:

'What is *Comploter* preparing?'

So the Duchess of Chevreuse took the face of the Duke of La Rochefoucauld in her hands and gently kissed the wound before she proceeded, slipping along as gently to the flesh of the lips.

*

When the Duchess of Chevreuse grasped the hand of the Duke of La Rochefoucauld, Esprit said that *Comploter* seduced *Ferus*.

They let their horses roam.

*

They are still trotting under the cluster of trees.

In front of the basin, they get down from their horses.

They walk, reaching the trees and the shade. They are in Couzières Park. The Duke hugs her whom he called *Disorder is Woman*.

*

Even as Lucilius had Seneca, La Rochefoucauld had Esprit.

Esprit wrote: Il n'y a que le coup en robbe. (This old proverb, in Old French, meant: There is pleasure only when it is stolen.)

*

'Comploter' means travelling under false names;

riding a horse after nightfall;

never opening the shutters.

It implies making love with a handkerchief in the mouth.

'Comploter' means hurrying away from the glow of the hearth in inns, from the torches in churches;

eating silently in one's room while wiping away, with every mouthful, the traces on the surface of the table.

Drinking each gulp of pure wine with still-breathless lungs, the heart beating at top speed.

It means pulling the shutters over the leather deadlights set high on the coach doors.

'Comploter' means being afraid to light one's Givet clay pipe, it means maintaining only a sooty flame, reading in the corner of a black wall, smelling strong, relieving oneself hastily and with the worry of being interrupted.

Desiring the woman whom one mustn't desire in a place where one mustn't do so.

Adultery.

Dipping one's tongue into that which it mustn't be dipped.

Touching one's sexual organ and pulling on it so strongly as if one had the intention of tearing it off and sending it flying into the rest of the surroundings.

'Comploter' means being afraid, adoring being afraid, being on the lookout everywhere,

more than reading,

it means deciphering all the letters that are not for oneself, transposing everything into its cipher, preparing an even more unforeseeable adventure, deciphering the message once it has been learnt by heart, swallowing the whole pieces of the letter on the spot.

CHAPTER 38

There are so few tyrannicidal ideas. There are so few thoughts that respond to order by refusing order, by overturning the syntactic arrangement, by distancing discursive argumentation. Thought must be capable of disobeying everything on which depend thinking, pensiveness, pendency, dependence. As it turned out, Étienne de La Boétie *wasn't even* published by Montaigne. Montaigne lacked the courage to do so. Montaigne lacked even the friendship to do so. Why, when I was a little child, was I the very refusal to eat, the refusal to speak, the refusal to answer the question, the refusal to subject myself to order or, rather, to the summoning of order? The desire to die rather than obey?

*

Phaedrus recounts in one of his most beautiful fables that a kid goat, having leapt onto the terrace of a farm, shouted abuse at a wolf that was lying down below with a wounded paw.

Under the shower of insults and mockery, the wolf at last raised his eyes.

He simply said to the little kid goat: 'Hey, it's not you who are cursing me, it's your *topos*!' (It's your position.)

*

Like all families that had to deal with the French police during the last war, my family had both a moderate and an apprehensive assessment of the mission that it fulfilled.

If one loves reading books, when one goes a little further into the subject matter, the history of the French police has its roots so deeply implanted in the religious Inquisition that one is completely terror-stricken.

Spinoza had a motto engraved on the setting of his ring: Caute. (Beware.)

My family's motto could have been: Beware of the French Train Company (SNCF). Beware of the Parisian Metro Authority (RATP). Beware of gendarmes who ring the doorbell. Beware of 'Republican' 'Security' Squadrons (the CRS, the State Security Police). Think incessantly of Drancy, which follows Pantin, which precedes Roissy.

*

Functionaries are people who carry out functions that contribute to the functioning of the State. Functionaries are people thanks to whom the State functions in the state that it is in. Here, the French word 'state' has the Latin sense of 'status', such as is visible in the expression 'statu quo'. But the Latin formula, which is entirely derived from *statu quo* and seems so spatial, so marked off by borders, so surrounded by border guards, by mounted policemen, by Customs officers, is in fact completely temporal: *statu quo ante*. Functionaries have the responsibility of making the state of what is function so that what will be 'afterwards' is how it was 'before'.

*

Theorem.

On the surface of the earth, the state of the world being ignoble, the *statu quo* ante as well.

*

Tacitus: Hideous misery, a puking place for everyone, as the great take naps.

*

The impassioned contribution to the war effort, the praise of the sacrifice of each person for the survival of the every-one, the vigorous stimulation of the reasons to fight against each other, the doping of hatred, that is, of meaning, that is, of orientation, that is, of the future, such is the task incumbent on magistrates, philosophers, priests, historians, politicians, on all men 'of state'. Commit yourself! Sacrifice yourself! Give us reasons to hope! Motivate your death, found your sacrifice, argue for your elimination!

*

General policy according to Henri Michaux. De-familiarize yourself. De-nationalize yourself. De-condition yourself. De-humanize yourself.

Michaux's watchword: Take a breath of fresh air wherever possible. Run for your life.

CHAPTER 39

Petrarcha

At the beginning of the year 1305, Petrarch's mother, riding a mare bought on the Moroccan shore, crossed the ford of the Arno. The horse took fright. The servant who was carrying the child wrapped up in his arms was thrown off his horse. The horse saved itself by swimming over to the shore, left the water, snorted, but the servant and the child were submerged by the eddies. No one could see them any more.

Nothing rose to the surface of the river except for eddies and bursting air bubbles.

Some bargees, who happened to be in a fishing boat, rushed over. They dove into the Arno. They grasped them in the dark shadow where they were rolling, hoisted them up, carried them to the shore and laid them out in the soft tepid muddy dust.

This is how, for his entire life, the greatest and the most amazing of the Renaissance men of letters lived like a shipwrecked Ulysses.

Ulysses searching everywhere for Ithaca.

Aeneas shipwrecked on the sands of Carthage.

An exile, a wanderer who had to atone for his life by means of a journey.

Peregrinus ubique. Everywhere a traveller.

When he was once again thrown from a horse in Bolsena, his left leg so seriously wounded that he could no longer use it, Petrarch had himself driven in a coach all the way to Rome. Once he had been carried in an armchair up to his room, once he was lying in bed, he began his correspondence with Boccaccio, who was in Florence.

He never recovered; always limped; always wrote; wrote and limped. Rode a horse, vanished into the dark water, wrote and limped.

*

All his life, he invariably repeated that he would have preferred living in the Republic of Naples, in that splendid bay where paradise and hell lie side by side, in the shadow of the Erstwhile, in the shadow of the two-mouthed volcano.

Naples was the Ithaca of this Ulysses who wandered on horseback through Europe and spent most of his life in France, in a small house on a hillside, walking over the soft little blue hyacinths of the woods.

Sade, five hundred years later, a few kilometres from there, thought the same thing as his ancestor Petrarch. He wrote: I would have preferred living in the most beautiful and, by far, the most criminal bay of the world, in the affectionate company of volcanoes.

CHAPTER 40

La Boétie

We are born all of a sudden in the atmospheric air, dazzled by the sunlight, enslaved by the most humiliating dependencies.

Freedom is not a part of the essence of mankind.

So that the little child who has just cried out can survive, the originary distress imposes care, cleanliness, help, food, defence. That is, the originary distress imposes other people on he or she who has had no autonomy in its conception; it imposes a family, obedience, fear, a common language, religion, rearing, the social convention of clothing, the arbitrary character of education, the tradition of culture, belonging to a nation. All this strange 'help' plunges the child into a mixture of love and hatred towards the brand-new father and with respect to the mother-source who has expulsed him into the light and given up breathing. It is a mixture of admiration and wound, at once desiring the other person and being desired by the other person, capturing without taking, pursuing without killing, desiring everyone's desire, killing without the act being seen, stealing everything.

An originary bond binds human beings together: the guilt commemorating the dream of a crime committed against the other person. The love for the Father is called politics. Putting him to death is called history. The individual soul is summed up as the guilt (having loved one's mother, having killed one's father, having devoured all the wild animals, having eaten the nature in these animals, these fish, these birds, these fruits, these roots, having stolen the heritage). Everyone's inflexible destiny is an endless conflict between everyone. In families, in couples, in groups, everything is torn apart, and, as it is being torn, enters into even greater opposition. The war without a truce between neighbouring nations, the never-ending war between two differing sexes, the civil war becoming at the end internal and confined inside oneself until it becomes anguish.

*

Twelve horses neigh. An old man and a young man come to a halt. This crossroads is eternal. Every horse paws the ground, its hooves in the air in broad sunlight. It's noon. The god of the daylight, in the highest part of the sky, loosens the reins. A son refuses to let his father go by. Such is every childhood and such is the history of the world.

*

Étienne de La Boétie wrote in his *Discourse on Voluntary Servitude*: I do not know why human beings do not have the force to desire freedom.

Why don't human beings have the force to desire freedom? Because being on the alert for death haunts the subject ever since his birth: from the moment when, alone, left to himself, he would be dead.

*

Freud thought that all human beings, from the onset of language on their lips, that is, from the dawn of society, were a band of murderers who lied.

Civil peace emerges when the fight to the death between groups finds itself in an exact equilibrium. Then the extreme tension of the rope sings. May brother hurl himself against brother. Frater in fratrem ruat! If neither of the two parties takes the advantage over the other one, if no one attempts to put an end to the carnage, then the land prospers.

What humanity describes of social functioning is always pure lying that is always putting up a screen.

Sade: Atheism is the explosion of the representation that societies make of themselves.

He lived imprisoned for thirty years.

Blanqui lived imprisoned for thirty-five years.

They are strange martyrs for a freedom in which they could take pleasure for only a few moments.

Frankly useless—and in this respect, mysterious—victims of a sacrifice that they should have avoided like the plague if they had had more duplicity, more importance, less virtue and heart.

Themselves, oddly voluntary victims.

When Étienne de la Boétie theorizes civil disobedience in 1548, he writes: I don't even ask you to make power tremble, but only not to support it any more.

Begin by stopping to vote for your enemies. Stop giving yourself masters. Stop paying supervisors to spy on you. Stop offering to the prince, by means of your work, the gold and the armies of which you will subsequently be victims. Stop giving the list of your possessions to those who insist on plundering you. Why do you form those lines that go up to the stake and feed the sacrifice for a few people or for only one person? Why are you so attached to being the favourite accomplice of murder and the faithful friend of despair? Animals would not bear what you consent to. Serve no longer.

*

The emperor Alexander put his hand on the wall, leaned on it, and bent down towards the poorest of men who had not even a platter for eating, not even a bowl for drinking, who drank simply from the cupped hollow of his palm, and he said to him:

'Ask me for whatever you want.'

Diogenes raised his head and replied to the emperor (the individual responded to power):

'Stand out of my sunlight.'

CHAPTER 41

The Noise of Freedom

There is a noise of freedom.

The noise of pinecones ripping open suddenly, beneath the branches, in the marvellous black shade of a parasol pine, across from the island of Capri, in summer, at Ischia, under a blue sky.

CHAPTER 42

Ovid

Anthropomorphosis is not finished.

Man cannot be defined without turning him into a prey for man.

The humanist question—'What is man?'—expresses a mortal danger.

If one formulates the wish not to exterminate human beings who do not respond to their religious, biological, social, philosophical, scientific, linguistic, sexual definitions, then man must be given up on as incomprehensible.

Ovid: Man must be given up on as non-finite, that is, as belonging to a species in the process of an infinite metamorphosis in a Nature that is itself an infinite metamorphosis.

CHAPTER 43

General Theory of Political Commitment

Beginning in 1880, Elisabeth Nietzsche-Förster was a committed woman, an engagée. With her husband, and an undeniable courage, she founded the *Germania* Camp in Paraguay to better the species and to change all men into super-men.

In 1933, Elisabeth Nietzsche-Förster walked across the salon of the Chancellery. Shaking, leaning on an old cane, she approached Adolf Hitler.

When she had arrived in front of him, she suddenly held out the old cane, on which she had been leaning, to the Chancellor, who took a step backwards.

'Mein Führer, es ist mir eine Ehre Ihnen den Spazierstock meines toten Bruders Friedrich zu schencken.' (Your Excellency, it is an honour for me to offer you this cane which my brother used when he was walking in the countryside.)

*

During the reign of Louis XIII, an 'engagé' meant a hired killer.

*

'Engagé' is to 'gage' (wage) what 'soldat' (soldier) is to 'solde' (pay).

Soldiers were, first and foremost, *enrôlés* (enrolled), that is, listed by writing on a roll as were the slaves in Ancient Roman times on latifundia.

Like domestic animals, the herds of the Neolithic period were branded with a letter by their first owner (to pen them in, to ride them, to sell them so that they would be imprisoned once again behind new palisades and killed, to cut them up, to roast them, to eat them).

*

As opposed to functionaries, who function, resignees, who resign, are men who tear themselves away from the social mission that had been allotted to them within a group in which they earned their livelihood.

Losing their wages, they become payless, that is, they cease to be, all of a sudden, soldiers who are 'engagés'.

Losing their pay ('soldes'), they become role-less.

Leaving society, they become asocial.

Ferenczi wrote: Sleep is the most asocializing act.

By leaving on the eve, one leaves the edge.

Every day we need to come back, whether we like it or not, into the lap of night, dream, desire.

Freud wrote: Sexual enjoyment is asocial. Every ejaculation weakens the need for society. The frequency of pleasure increases individualism. Sexual inhibition favours obedience to the authority of the group.

Freud dared to write: With daily sexual satisfaction, a child could not be educated.

*

Men or women of letters, because this word refers to human beings who decompose all things letter by letter and all relations fragment by fragment, are human beings who break the path.

They scissor all the strings. They climb the old ramparts of the park in which they have been locked up, no matter what one does to restrain them. They hoist themselves over the walls of the barracks. They turn themselves back into savages. They are like cats who prefer gutters to salons; they wander, timid, subtle, withdrawing at the slightest sound, thrown by the slightest pain, springing at the slightest movement of a gossamer thread, of a passing cloud, of a flitting bee, of a falling leaf, neglecting railroads, airports, tollways, heading over the steep, slick slate roofs, through the muddy ditches of fields, across the wet foggy shores of streams.

*

Lancelot says:

'Prepare my horse.'

'Why?'

'It's because suddenly I feel that my body is impatient to be here no longer.'

Impatience can be summed up thus: break here.

Make time of space.

When I was a child, I would withdraw to the back of the parish priest's garden of the Maurepas Church, in the shadow of the half-ruined tower that dated from the Hundred Years' War. Sheltered by the gooseberry bushes, I would read, in an armchair covered with dusty upholstery, books which were still bound in white or rose cloth and which had been collected by my great-grandfather. Then I would get up, hoist myself over the sheet-metal roof of the shed, sit down, hidden by the branches of the trees, on the round-topped low wall that separated the parish priest's garden from the chapel of the monument to the dead of the Franco-Prussian War of 1870, on which had been added the names of the soldiers who had perished in the trenches of 1914. This low wall was like a horse taking me very far. I would sit straight on it, stiff like a knight of the Round Table who had donned his most beautiful suit of armour for his next tournament, his soul keen on extraordinary adventures. I would dream about my life. Five years later, in the park of Sèvres, beyond the Japanese bridge drawn by Gustave Kahn, I would saddle myself on a similar wall, which had hidden Madame de Pompadour's loves but which was completely covered with ivy and less pleasant to my bare thighs under my flannel shorts because of the greasy, thick, green, dusty leaves that made of the ivy a kind of sad, dark, bad-luck token. This is how I rode my horse forth motionlessly in my life, astride nothing, as can happen when one desires.

CHAPTER 44

Reading

When the Sun Horse, in the Vedic world,

    stops for a moment,

    at noon,

    to drink,

    the reins fall.

    It's the unharnessing-for-a-moment in the sky.

    Time sometimes unharnesses.

    Reading unharnesses.

    Time exploded in the depths of the sky long before the
sun shined.

    It continues.

    And the sun shined long before there were eyes.

    It continues.

    The subject matter of this scene has no anecdote.

    It is always this sudden state of looking out,

    immobile,

    silent,

    in the light,

    of two bodies,

    of which one falls.

CHAPTER 45

The Horse of Time

Upanishad I: the horse is the image of time, the year is its body, the sky its back, the dawn its dishevelled head as it emerges from night.

Rig Veda, XIX: For the Name-that-precedes-the-first-of-the-gods is concentrated in the Time-that-irradiates-the sky.

There is no end to the universe where this fire snorting and unfurling like a reddish gold mane rouses and metes.

And there is no programme in what life one day tested blindly on the little matter that it modified discontinuously.

The non-programme, the unprogrammable, the unpre-dictable—such are the explosive depths of temporality.

This falls like a lightning bolt; this swoops down like an eagle; this overturns the prediction; every true thought unsaddles the curious inhabitant of the soul, colonized by language, submerged by dream, oriented by hunger, driven wild by desire.

*

Plato: Aporia means no longer knowing which way to turn one's mind (no longer knowing which way to go forward inside the mind). The little angel of the soul is often immobilized on the spot. He finds himself without the slightest resources. Thus, in Greek, aporia becomes apeiria. The awkward position becomes infinite.

*

During copulation, the 'ride' is not only an image. In horse riding, the ride is itself a simile. Equus eroticus is represented on the walls of human beings and in dreams before the domestication of Equus caballus.

*

When the 'ride' has vanished, the lovers, completely naked, lying on their backs in bed, unsaddled by time, which has ecstatically raised them for a moment, which has suddenly fled from their surroundings, even as their dream has also faded away within their bodies, unharness themselves.

The genitals of one of them have shrivelled up.

The dark lips of the other one have dried up.

The arms still thrown back are de-symbolized in the distress of a desire that is no longer possible for their bodies, nor even comprehensible as a desire in the depths of the soul.

*

When lovers have a horse ride, they gallop in another world.

The time they dissolve is their joy.

And only happiness in person, irradiating from their depths, is capable of unsaddling their lovemaking.

It comes. Time is like pleasure. It comes from behind the world. It comes from something that is upstream from each body. And it surges.

It comes and, when it is there, once it has arrived, what has arrived has arrived without one's waiting for it.

Pleasure is at once *as intrusive as it is expected*.

Even as sexual enjoyment 'gathers speed' and 'over-comes' the desire to be finished with desire, *time* defines the *speed* that catches unawares the *rhythm* of what surges forth, downstream from space.

*

During the embrace that adjoins the bodies to the instant of the sexual act, the souls of the woman and the man experience a crisis within their respective identities. They both experience an extraordinary, heartrending, incurable impression. It is an animalistic sharing that cannot truly be shared within linguistic sharing which is, itself, a genuine dialogue where all the anatomical differences vanish. Linguistic sharing opposes an entirely interchangeable 'I' and a 'you' in the dialogue whereas the sexual organ of one person is not interchangeable with the sexual organ of the other person in the desire that animates reproduction.

Both cling to each other. Both want their excitement to last. Both want the end of their excitement. Both wanting to unite in an explosion of sensual delight, they hug, fit themselves together, kiss, hastening each other to attain it. Of course, even as they do everything to finish the act, they don't want this end to be tristitia, a slackening, a swelling down, disgust. However, wanting the end to be voluptuous, they provoke this incredible détente, this release through pulling the stopper, this emptying out, this a-symbolic void, this languidness that they open in front of themselves.

Because they want the opposite of joy by desiring to enjoy an orgasm, their sexual enjoyment starts the distress into which they fall, squealing.

Sexual intercourse is a crisis of time.

One of them wants the most extreme haste; the other one, to temporize as long as possible.

One wants to see as if in a dream, explosively (rapid eye movement). The other wants to sink into slow waves, like happiness seeping into sand (like that sand leading to Damas, beneath the horseshoes of a horse that trotted on through the calm daylight, where a body is overturned, where eyes close).

*

Sexual disparities are very strange saddles.

Strange saddles because, from the instant that they no longer take sexual enjoyment out of desiring, from the instant that they desire to have sexual enjoyment, *it is the sexual intercourse itself that unsaddles the bodies by means of these two directly opposable parts of the bodies.*

This experiment is performed by two people (and a genuine two, man and woman not being *idems* as in language, but rather *alters* as is indicated so visibly by those 'strange saddles' located approximately at the centre of their bodies).

I am evoking a temporal modality which doesn't last and which, however, is much vaster and substantial than an instant.

1. The ordeal that there is no infinity in that which is ulterior. 2. The ordeal that finitude is bewitching.

*

I would like to underscore a third point. There is never a present in the fundamental human experience which, from tome to tome, from wall to wall, from fragment to fragment, from book to book, from stage to stage, from image to image, I seek to describe because it reproduces mankind. In two ways. 1. 'I wish it had lasted' did not belong to the temporal modality of the present indicative. 2. Even more: 'I wish it had lasted' de-fines the non-in-finiteness of the non-present of the present.

It is *to ti ên einai.*

It is this 'past still moving in the state of the past' in the actuality of the act.

Most concretely, according to the terms of the Orient: There exists a 'protention', an anticipation of desire, which is a retention of sexual enjoyment.

The Taoist hermits of China, then the denuded Tantric men of India, in their noetic and erotic asceticism, said that this ordeal is both the most painful and the most sublime.

The same is true of the masochists of monarchist, then colonialist, then industrial Europe.

It is said that a woman who was a dancer would have a ride on Aristotle. Her name was Campaspe. She would put the bit between his teeth. This is how the philosopher who founded the metaphysics of the ancient Greeks came to desire.

Strange aorist that persists in the depths of being, in Aristotle's strange 'unmoved mover'.

Love is a tragic temporality.

So that what has advanced doesn't advance, so that the expiration doesn't expire, so that the pressure does not get depressed, the several spasms characteristic of the bewitching finitude of sexual intercourse 'form' human rhythmics. Duple or triple or quadruple or quintuple time is the rhythm of voluptuousness. It is not a present if it is a rhythm. It is not 'one' beat, not one 'time', if it is not a present. Man does not know the 'one'-beat rhythm, 'one' time'. Those from whom his body proceeds do not know 'one' ejaculation. Those from whom his body proceeds do not form 'one' body. The origin does not know 'one' Big Bang, but rather a slow implosion in which the explosions, before they happen, have their source.

The ancient Romans strangely defined this temporal experience that represented the duration of a metamorphosis, which established the referent of every mutation, by saying that *voluptas* is a *taedium vitae*. That the orgasm is a kind of disgust at life. A de-fascination. At the moment when it happens, the reproduction of life un-leashes and un-veils its death's-face. Life comes to be dis-gusted at itself during the greatest of its joys, which is the very one in which it is re-leashed and will be re-vived in the form of other bodies surging forth into time, nine lunar months later, to pick back up the name of the dead person who precedes it. From this bitterness in the very interior of pleasure is born the *tristitia*, which is the unexcitableness of desire, the falling asleep of the soul, dreaming and just as soon, in the dream, the regretted desire, the hallucination of sexual enjoyment leading to genital re-excitement, which is a carnal more than a corporal restoration.

But this nostalgia is also indexed and, once again, mysterious: the regret that recalls the joy of the previous tension implies the opposite of a present. To understand the Roman aporia that makes a disgust at life out of the pleasure of life reproducing itself, to ex-plicate the im-plication of a desire seeking its disgust, to un-pleat entirely this recapitulation or this re-crouching of the body by means of desire, this must be said: a 'Jadis', an Erstwhile, inhabits voluptuousness as a deficiency of excitement. This deficiency is the excitement characteristic of the waiting for the orexis. The surging forth prefers itself to abandonment, twilight, autumn, death. Frustration founds the soul because the originary loss is this foundation bringing back incessantly the natal distress during sexual life. In the sudden assuagement, there is no longer a 'to-come'. No longer finding any accessible voluptuousness, nor even an available voluntary image, nor an unexpected phantasm, nor a dream, the whole body ceases to be 'alive'; it is unsaddled; it is dis-oriented.

Once assuaged, every body is *in the past*.

Something of the Without-Antecedent despairs there. Voluptuousness castrates the sexual organ. What is originary is then *absolutely* lost. It is the pure Erstwhile that then deserts for an instant, in the depths of the sexual night.

It is not only the lost erection: it is the 'perdu', that which has been lost—'the lost'—that takes over.

That which has been *lost* at birth and completely *re-lost* at the end of intercourse, such is the strange and so ill-named masculine human pleasure—sudden, subito, exaiphnès.

*

Position of ecstasy: position of death.

It's opisthotonus.

Such is Saint Paul's *conversion* in the staggering image invented by Caravaggio (who was the greatest inventor of staggering nocturnal imagery in European history, after the origin of nocturnal imagery during prehistory) to give an account for it.

The scenes that Caravaggio invents have the nocturnal force of dreams that visit animals without mastering them.

The scenes offended his contemporaries, but they immediately fascinated.

Everyone suddenly recognized what he had long been waiting for, in what Caravaggio was doing.

*

Head and trunk violently overturned, arms extended behind the head—opisthotonus subdivides into three worlds: trance, tetanus, hysteria. These are the three worlds of the shamans. When bisons die, they seem to be shamans in a trance because this retrocephalic contraction characterizes the death of bisons.

It is the admirable overturning of the emotion of gratitude.

Dogs zoologically turning over on the tiled floor, cats on sofas, men and women in beds whenever they would like to be seized by sexual enjoyment. A passive disposition that opens the flesh and offers it to penetration. It is not certain that this position, which is devoted to an effraction, is not engendered by a turning-over reflex originating far upstream from humanity. One suddenly sees horses in a meadow that turn over on their backs in this way and offer themselves. Offer themselves to what? To nothing. To the sun above them, to the wind blowing by, or rubbing their back in the grass or in the sand, the thistles, the pebbles.

CHAPTER 46

Like Orpheuses who have re-climbed the path from the Underworld, have suddenly cried out again at the end of the desire re-born again in the light, it is as re-livers in this world who have re-become brutally and completely alone—and are plunged into mourning for a life that we have lived in another world from which we have emerged with difficulty—that we live.

'Re' constitutes the heart.

We re-live.

By dint of being enigmatic, re-cognition recognizes nothing of what it sees anew.

One fine day, re-cognition admits to being pure Discovering.

The other sexual organ can become a 'piece of knowledge', 'something one knows', which does not mean that the other sexual organ can ever be known by the other sexual organ.

The other sexual organ ever remains, however near one can come to it, however denuded it can be under one's fingers, however examined it can be under worried or attentive eyes, an inaccessible reality.

It is as this external object inaccessible to the inner experience of he or she who has the other sexual organ that it fascinates, and that the impossible perceptual invasion takes place even in phantasms and dreams.

The pensive knight leaning on the windowsill contemplates the queen who is going away; suddenly he topples over, falls out of the window, he is going to die—but Gawain retains him.

Then a new life begins.

'Re' returns.

For Lancelot, for Abelard, for Paul, for Petrarch, for Montaigne, for Brantôme, for d'Aubigné, etc.—they fell off their horses, had the feeling of having slid into death, but suddenly they sense themselves returning from the other world. They have returned to this world. Their hands grip something. Writers are the twice alive.

CHAPTER 47

The Praying Mantis

Opisthotonos indicates the appearance of the deadly spectre of the praying mantis when it is aggressed.

The abdomen is arched up; the thorax trembles; the wings make a noisy rubbing sound; concealed up to now, two postiche eyes, at the base of the arms, half open; these *postiche* eyes are two white, black-rimmed spots that stare wide-eyed.

There is something exact to say of the women and men who are in a trance: their elytra topple upwards.

The thorax pushes the legs to the sides and towards the back—legs which are called 'human' to cast light on sight that sees nothing.

CHAPTER 48

Opisthotonoses of Aelios the Rhetor

He embarked in Ostia during the celebration of the Ludi Apollinares (13 July 144). He left Pavras when the days equalled the nights (22 September 144). The sailing was stormy. The galley prudently kept close to the coasts of Sicily. The first opisthotonos took place in front of Cephalonia. Aelios writes that, when they reach the Aegean Sea, it was not his body that arched backwards, but the boat itself which overturned in the wind. At last, after one final storm that lasted fourteen days, when Miletus could be spotted, the great ancient rhetor could no longer unfold his legs, could no longer walk, could no longer progress by putting down his hind legs on the ground. His slaves placed him on a litter. They carried him, his arms remaining thrown backwards, his fingers curved, ready to claw. It was then that Aelios discovered that he had become a little deaf. He travelled like this, tense, always lying on his back, progressing in short stages. It was impossible for him to read in this position. He thus had his books read to him by a Gallic slave who remained near him and was obliged to shout slowly each word into his ear.

At the beginning of winter, he was in Smyrna. The doctors, the gymnasts, the oniromants, the sortilegi surrounded him. They auscultated him. They experienced real difficulties in choosing among the multitude of medical problems with which they saw him overwhelmed. Because he had all the illnesses, they diagnosed nothing in particular and prescribed a cure at the hot springs of the Meles River.

This was the moment chosen by the goddess Isis to send her sacred geese to him. The warning took place during his cure. He had recovered much of his hearing. Aelios found himself turned over on a warm stone inside the thermal baths. But Aelios did not recognize the goddess at the instant when the geese flew across the sky, although he had distinctly heard their frightening honking. Not only did he not recognize the sign hidden behind the geese, he also omitted to have the dream analysed that he had during the night that followed that visions. Moreover, he forgot the dream. He reproached himself for this so sharply that he began to keep a diary. Beginning with his sojourn at the thermal baths of Meles River, Aelios dictated all the dreams that he recalled upon awakening, striking with his cane the young Gallic slave who was from the north of the Loire River, from the region of Routot, and who would remain lying below the bed so that, while Aelios was still affected by his dream, he could take it down in 'stenographic notes' on the wax of a boxwood tablet. Aelios was staying in the house of a neokoros.

In this diary, he lists the names of his companions at the thermal-bath cure (he prefers to speak of incubants or incubi) who lived in the same house as he did, located inside the Asklepieion: the philosopher Rhosandros, the senator Salvius Julianus, the senator Sedatus, the charming philosopher Evarestos, the poet Bibulus, and Hermocratos of Rhodes.

All of them communicated their dreams and *shelled* them—according to Aelios—like *precious peas*.

The end of November was splendid. God successively appeared to him in five different forms: a mote of dust visibly increasing in size, in a ray of sunlight, like a kind of lead ball, while he was taking a mud bath; an atrocious childhood memory because of the stench of a particularly ripe fig while he was eating a meal; a fever blister on his forehead after eating pork; a complicated pun that had the form of an inextricable riddle; a belch that was almost like a song. He then experienced a period of overwork. Not only the god Asklepios appeared to him in every place, in all circumstances, by night and by day, indicating to him the best medications and lavishing advice, but Telesphoros also visited him. Then it was Sarapis. One day, Athena came to find him when she had taken on the form of Phidias' statue and was thus standing completely motionless before his eyes in a clearly hostile posture. Another day, it was Hermes, in the guise of Plato, and it was pure luck that Aelios did not confuse them. Then came Demosthenes, disguised as Lysia, and Sophocles, disguised as the emperor Hadrian. Aelios notes that living like this is no longer living; it means telling a difficult, endless dream. Every day he lists tumours, breathlessness, spitting up blood, paralyses of his face, ankyloses of his neck, rheumatism in his hands, attacks of opisthotonos that arch his body backwards on the marble pavement, on the multicoloured pebbles, on the Syrian rug. He said that not only these contractions stiffened his body backwards, like the priestesses of Apollo when they entered into a trance, but also that his spine became so curved that his companions had the impression that he had become like a ship's sail bellowed by the wind. Never, he wrote, had the neokoroses, the religious officials and the incubi ever seen attacks of opisthotonos as arched as his. At last he dies, a little after this; he gives out a last breath—as we all do—in an opisthotonic position. He is like Enguerrand Quarton's *Dead Christ* of 1456. He is like my dead grandmother, whom I loved so much, to whom I owe my having continued to live, when she was stretched out, arched back, on the floor of the apartment of the rue Marié-Davy in 1986.

CHAPTER 49

Delilah

The Blinding of Samson was painted by Rembrandt during the year 1636. One has the impression that the Biblical hero is just inside the opening of a cave from which he wants to leave. There is an immense movement of several bodies all astride each other on the *threshold of light*. To tell the truth, it's a terrible nativity scene. It's the Thirty Years' War that has become a painting. Samson has been turned over on his back in an opisthotonic position by a soldier who has traitorously grasped him and who is below him. In front of him is a Philistine priest wearing a turban, with Turkish-style baggy pants, threatening him with a halberd whose iron is also as arched as Samson's back can be. A third soldier, wearing a shiny breastplate, plunges his dagger into Samson's eye and begins the first enucleation. A fourth soldier already fetters his wrist to the millstone in Gaza, where his strength will finally be domesticated. A fifth soldier brandishes high in the air an almost useless sword— so many soldiers are there to make Samson a prisoner—but it indicates the desire that they cannot assuage. On the far-left side (one reads from left to right in Europe), on the credence, held down by a gold wine pitcher, the blue purse contains the 1,100 shekels paid for the betrayal.

Delilah is getting ready to flee through the luminous opening.

She is the only one completely standing in the luminous opening.

She is gripping, in her left hand, the seven braids of long reddish blond hair destined for God, a mane which up to then has never been touched by an iron razor and in which resides all the irresistible muscular power of the hero.

The still-open scissors sparkle in her right hand.

*

The scene of the Tears of Saint Peter is already present in Judges XVI.

The scene of the Tears of Saint Peter is this: 'Before the cock crow twice, *thou shalt deny me thrice.*' This is what God had told him expressly (expressis verbis). The apostle stands in the nocturnal courtyard. He is looking at the fire. He is weeping.

The scene that is the source of the scene with Peter during the Passion of Jesus in the New Testament is specifically the scene with Delilah bent over Samson in the Old Testament. Delilah suddenly starts shouting. She says to Samson: 'How canst thou say, I love thee, when thine heart is not with me? *Thou hast mocked me these three times.*' Quomodo dicis quod amas me? Per tres vices mentitus es mihi.

Then Samson weeps. He draws towards him the face of the young woman whom he loves. He succumbs to her shouts. He kisses the lips of the young woman; he confides in her the secret of his force:

'There hath not come a razor upon mine head [. . .] if I be shaven, then my strength will go from me, and I shall become weak, and be like any other man.'

Delilah then leans back on the bedpost of the sumptuous bed, near the lamp. She softly takes her lover's cheeks between her hands; she places his face on her stomach; she puts him to sleep like a child.

With Samson's head sunk super genua sua, the young woman softly arranges his locks one by one on her thighs.

She waits until he has fallen asleep.

She listens to him sleeping.

While his appeased breathing is making his chest softly rise and fall, she beckons the warriors to enter.

And, while by candlelight they cut the seven locks off the head of the man who continues to sigh and sleep on her knees, she dreams of what she will be able to buy with the 1,100 shekels that she will receive.

*

Behind Delilah's body standing in the light, there is a lamp whose flame is reflected on the scissors held in her hand.

For Peter, it's a brazier, and he reaches out his frozen fingers to its rim.

For light, we use what shines brightest in this world, greatly outshining scissor blades, courtyard braziers, even the filaments of the electric light bulbs that hang from the ceiling, even the sun high in the sky.

For light, we use *firebrands of active hate*.

Envy is like the lantern held by Judas during the Night of Agony.

At the age of fifty, Sigismund Freud began to write fairy tales. One day, the brothers gathered. They wondered:

'Why not kill our father?'

So they killed him. They ate him. The taste was good. They sucked all the bones. They piously sucked up all his brains. Time passed, their satiety passed.

Oddly, their jaws seemed to hurt.

'Re-morse' seized them in the lower part of their faces, in a very mysterious way, as if they were 're-biting', more or less at the place where, sunken in and jutting forward, stand the teeth that bite the Fathers.

CHAPTER 50

Plutarch wrote: How brave was the first man who neared his mouth to death! What virtue was his when he ripped the flesh that he had wounded, when his ivory teeth broke the bones on which his prey would stand and when he sucked the marrow that they concealed! When he put inside himself the parts of a body that once had neighed, barked, bleated, bellowed, roared, how did their memory, their image, their pain, their gaze, their blood, not turn his stomach and heart?

But the heart is not turned.

It beats more strongly.

Horror excites humanity.

Not only does the spectacle of horror not turn one away from what is displayed, but also the ceremony of what terrifies attracts populations in mass, arranges their footsteps into a march, unites them into a nation.

No perfected torture has ever given the torturer who conceived it such enjoyment that it quenched his curiosity for the new kind of suffering that he imagines almost as soon, and that he notes down in the notebook in which he records those he has killed.

The millions of victims over the thousands of centuries have rarely dreamt of taking to their heels, failing to have, as far as they were concerned, the slightest suspicion of what awaited them. They keep screaming on the spot because they are hypnotized by the aggressiveness martyring them. This aggressiveness is the uninhibited desire for death. Killing each other off is the specific passion of the *homo* species, making its black blood, its viruses, its *virtus*, surge forth, as opposed to other wild animals for which predation is simply a state of being famished for the prey that will satisfy their appetite, and thus a state as immediately assuaged as it had been specifically famished. The hundreds of millions of screens that cover the planet have become the new fascinator organ, replacing sacrifices and rites, crowds on pilgrimages, masses trampling the ground. This is the final step in sedentarization. It is the pogrom that has become immobile. Although the spectacle does not entirely appease the horrified enjoyment that it excites, it at least nails to the ground the spectator who scrutinizes the flowing blood. Those whom it dumbfounds are turned into prey by the spectacle, with addresses, identity cards, banker's cards—numbered victims, sitting, petrified bodies likely to be racketeered and pillaged. One's stunned state is offered up for grabs to everyone else. Once hatred has become immobile to this extent, it is transformed into fear. Fear, that unique companion of desire, as it is confined to a sedentary state and private property, is reprocessed into anguish. This anguish seeks protection from the power that it has itself delegated, in a nerve-racking experience, to counter its dread, to whom it consents as if it were not its belonging in the form of obedience, ravaged freedom, physical immobility, social spinelessness. What democracies call politics, ever since the beginning of this century, neglecting the horror of the century that preceded this new century, is in the process of committing the fault of criminalizing the protest on which they are founded and which should shake them into a *tumult* in order to keep them alive.

CHAPTER 51

Hannah Arendt's Sorites

The more civilized a society is, the more ancient are the traces that its memory has preserved. The more numerous and varied the traces of its history, the richer and more diverse the symbolic world that it opens out. The more fertile and unpredictable the symbolic world, the more ingenious and, as it were, visionary the human beings who invent new objects. The more the human beings who work increase in number the technical feats and distribute these ever more perfected objects, the more individuals, once they have returned to their private world, deep inside themselves, become sensitive to something that they have not produced.

The more they are attracted by everything that is simply given.

The more they marvel at nature.

The more wildness fascinates them.

The more uninhibited cruelty beckons to them, obsesses them, inebriates them.

CHAPTER 52

A domesticated species going back to its wild state is said to be feral.

*

What do you mean by the moral penchants of the human species? The extermination of wild animals? The invention of slavery? Crucifixion? The invention of work? War? The Polish camps? The camps in Siberia? The mass graves of Rwanda? The metallic shelves of Cambodia?

CHAPTER 53

The Silent Core

The first human beings were reunited by an insurmountable horror precisely bearing upon what had primitively been the attractive centre of their union. It is this return, to them—first oneiric, then figurative, then linguistic—to the violent death of the wild animals that they had hunted by *imitating* the wild animals that hunted them—that turned their souls into a satellite revolving around a kind of minimal 'return-image', a torque, a 're-morse', literally, a 're-bite' in the depths of their hunger, well before a core of conscience is formed.

It is a *silent core*.

A core initially mortal (which sustains them). Then, long afterwards, a sexual core (which reproduces them).

Georges Bataille spoke of the *region of oppressed silence* that is established around the dead body that is eaten by the wild animals, even as it is abruptly established in front of the tiny feminine hole through which passes the body, which is being reborn, of all mammals.

What Noah's cloak hides is his erect sexual organ (social reproduction). But what is hidden in Ham's cloak is Nimrod the Hunter (total hunting).

Total hunting defines the ancient human world from ~80,000 to ~10,000. This is by far the longest period of human history. One calls prehistory the extremely long history of the extermination of the big wild animals. This is the genuine *silent core* of human societies. The silent core facing blood. The dead interval in which languages developed rapidly. The core of flesh-eating laughter blended with sexual fright in which this laughter is reproduced. The famished core of chewing that is fascinated, that is, mimetic. This is the Dionysian chant.

*

Joy has its source and even already takes a sample of its substance in the promise that arches the body.

The promise of pleasure is provoked by the spectacle of the prey that falls, that *separates* the teeth of he who watches it falling—falling and being born form the embryo of dance.

I do not hold laughter in great esteem because it breaks the seal of the smile.

All laughter hates what is weakest.

Thin lips, such as those on the statues from Cartoceto, are called 'Cicero's lips'.

Curled-up lips after the fashion of the hitch that grips the saddle, and the unsaddling that ensues, until the mastication that little by little introduces one into the invisible world.

*

First of all, we were little mammals, the prey of reptiles. Then forest creatures with very small prehensile hands, intermittently standing, in a state of pure alertness, like felines trembling on their hind legs and troubling themselves about everything that happens, with facial eye sockets, with stereoscopic vision, the incessant prey of birds and wild animals. When the continents drifted to the north, all the primates emigrated to the south: they pursued the sun that the plants, which one claims are sedentary, were also pursuing by moving. The almost-human animals are characterized by a dubious, non-instinctive gregariousness, instinct having been displaced into the post-natal acquisition by their offspring of cries and breathing and alerts and panicky fears and the more or less affectionate, more or less grumbling intonations of the mothers who fear for their survival and who enjoy the use of their empire.

As survival behaviour, the primal world returns: all human beings withdraw, avoid each other, move to outlying areas, become once again solitary individuals devoid of pity towards their fellow creatures and even towards their loves.

Beginning with the origin of human associations, social structure is polarized between anchorites (shamans, the insane, bachelors, adolescents, hunters in outlying areas) and the reproductive core most often dominated by males and the elderly but whose dominant characteristic is feminine.

Social time is polarized between the scattering of little spring-like cells whose renewal arouses and the regrouping of great wintery bands threatened by death.

I meditate on the extreme remains of the life led by the human beings who were deported into the camps of the Second World War. It is on this shore that I was born and that I have written. It is in this ruin that I have sought to re-live. I have blended these relics of distress with the lost mores of the most ancient societies. (With the lost mores of the Ik people.) I imagine the lifestyle of human beings in the Palaeolithic era during winter. The goal of the efforts made was not old age, not wealth, not even the dream of a poss-ible return to the quietude anterior to their birth. Not even vengeance. It did not even consist of attaining the next year.

They sought to attain the night, alive.

And in their dreams: having a mouth full of food during a great feast, remaining alive until the next spring, feeling the warmth of the first sunlight, seeing once again the miraculous sprouting of the vegetation and the berries to pick, wild beasts to kill and cleave with bits of broken bones or stone chips.

*

Beginning with birth, beginning with the unweaned-infant state, the body fears the law of an eye for an eye. This fear is pre-human. All dreaming animals have this dream. One who is bitten bites. One who is killed kills. Excrement buries. This inter-animal and international fear knows no subjective boundary.

CHAPTER 54

The Sharecropper's Wife from Rodez

In 1777, the court clerk of the seneschal of Rodez noted down the testimony of a sharecropper's wife. Her younger brother had just killed their elder brother. The sharecropper's wife had heard the rifle shot. A little later, while she was with her husband in the room, her younger brother pushed open the door. Here is the text, verbatim, of the clerk recording the testimony of the sharecropper's wife:

'Raymond came and sat down. Her husband told him that there were some people who would not eat the good pieces. He said yes. Her husband said that there were some people who had been lying in wait very early. Raymond didn't respond. Her husband said that were some people who would be hanged. Then Raymond said that a rifle shot was better. She told him that it would be better if rifles didn't exist. Raymond responded that if rifles didn't exist, then what happened wouldn't have happened.'

This deposition made by Raymond's sister to the seneschal of Rodez is a model for me.

The style of this text fascinates me in that (1) the narration excludes taking a direct part in what is said, (2) each person who speaks ferociously excludes directly challenging the person spoken to. In other words, according to the sharecropper's wife from Rodez, language restricts itself to (1) surrounding the reality with negations and images, (2) avoiding a puncturing of the non-verbal pouch concealed in the depths of each body. This shows 'pudeur', a sense of restraint, at the level of language. It is the anti-psychological style par excellence. One finds traces of this magnificent *restive rhetoric* when one reads the old Icelandic sagas. One unearths shreds of it in the anecdotes of Roman annals. Ancient Japanese tales recorded the short circuits of it before Nô theatre plays lay hold of it to make lyrical enigmas, and today's butoh dancing makes imagery out of it. However, in all the kinds of reading which I have done with delight, to which I have abandoned myself until I was dizzy, which make up, to my eyes, the deepest part of the library, nothing that I have found seems to me as striking as this single sentence that the sharecropper's wife from Rodez utters in her own name: 'She told him that it would be better if rifles didn't exist.' The clerk simply reports a dialogue that was reported to him. The clerk is like the servant woman in Emily Brontë's *Wuthering Heights*. He is like the guardian in Lycophron's *Cassandra*. He is the third person who makes the insane scene visible. Interrogated by the seneschal, the sharecropper's wife lets her husband speak as much as possible. But suddenly she can no longer support the pain; this is about her brother, who is only her husband's brother-in-law, and for her it is her brother who has killed her brother, and suddenly she explodes: she cries out that it would have been better if rifles had not existed. The sharecropper's wife pronounces these rather oneiric words while her elder brother has just died from a rifle bullet shot right into his head by her little brother Raymond. All the natural languages—which derive from dreams invented by the famished hallucinations of warm-blooded creatures—give rise to fictions. Language is an 'irréalisateur', it cannot make something real, even if its uttering has real effects. The ersatz in the form of little stubs of phrases surging forth has endless unpredictable consequences. The sharecropper's wife from Rodez shows more than a sense of restraint, more than circumspection. She shows much more than laconism. She avows the secret that language cannot make something real and that this secret constitutes the depths of the soul.

*

Moreover, I think that the attitude underlying the only sentence that the sharecropper's wife pronounced in her own name in front of the clerk of the Rodez court in 1777 goes still farther than a refusal to make any show of what is inside oneself. A faith is at stake. I think that what incites one to speak, in the way the sharecropper's wife gave testimony to the town clerk, is the belief that one must not entrust to language that which one experiences, that language is not good for the soul. It is to this faith that I want to dedicate this second-to-last loop of my poor realm of very small shores, of dismantled wharves, of towpaths invaded by brambles and mint, of broken gutters, of tidemarks, of shattered streets, of threatening ruins. This faith is the certitude that language does not originate in the soul and that it must constantly be reminded of this.

There is an incommunicable core. A judgement must be measured, psychism surrounded by walls, bombast excluded, tears held back, emotional demonstrations prohibited. The heart of the self must by no means be uncovered. A myth tells of an Inuit hunter who did not want to entrust his language with what he felt. Even when he was alone, he did not communicate his impressions to himself. So the hero invented a secret language with the intention of speaking to himself and of telling himself the truth without the spirit of the language understanding him. His name? Nukarpiatekak. I would need to find the trace of this myth in ice or snow. I would need to tear it out of Captain Cook. I would need to meditate more on this gap of every language. This *magical safeguarding* of what does not belong to the community is a marvellous, extrinsic consequence of language when it is acquired late. It is inner life considered as an absolute night. Even as inner animation was without language until the age of two, this life must remain sheltered from the spying of those who are nearby. Even more so, this life must maintain itself in the former silence in which it was constituted before the acquisition of the familial language by all the beings who dream in silence throughout the night. The soul is thus conceived like a world into which no one else can penetrate. Not even oneself by means of the language used by everyone. If speaking sends the body into hysterics, then it's out of the question to communicate one's secret *even to language*. There is a savagery that cannot be exploited and it alone enables the survivors to survive amid those who speak. At the end of childhood, the human body begins to believe in what it has learnt to say, the body begins to love its persecutor, the bird is beckoned by the air and the spider by the stream bank, the dreamer by nocturnal images, the rifle that does not exist by death within which nothing else exists.

CHAPTER 55

On Joseph

The definition of the functioning of human societies was given in the second book of the Torah. It is the unanimous cry made by Joseph's brothers: 'Come now therefore, and let us slay him!'

What is this word, in the text that is read during the liturgy, that reins over this scene? The word Occident.

Here is the text of Genesis translated by Saint Jerome. Saint Jerome translated the Bible from Hebrew and from Greek in the Palestine desert, in the solitude of a cave.

In the mountains, a man met up with a wanderer. He asked him:

'What are you seeking?'

'My brothers.'

The man looking for the brotherliness of his brothers was named Joseph. But his brothers saw him arriving from afar. They plotted his death (cogitaverunt illum *occidere*), saying among themselves:

'Come now therefore, and let us slay him!' (*Occidamus* eum!)

*

'Come now therefore, and let us slay him!' This 'heartfelt cry' can be found again in the extraordinary Gospels of the Christians, of which it makes up the main plot.

In the New Testament, this cry is addressed to God himself.

On 30 April, in front of the council of the Elders, in Jerusalem, facing Roman soldiers who were organizing the enchanting public spectacle of an execution, Caiaphas defines society when he repeats the cry, of Joseph's brothers, against Jesus then disguised, derisively, at least as he was judged by his persecutors, as the King of the Jews. Caiaphas declares deliberately: 'It is good that a man dies to prevent the loss of an entire people.' John writes in Greek: 'Hena anthrôpon apothanein hyper tou laou.' Jerome translates into Latin: 'Unum hominem mori pro popolo.' Thanks to Caiaphas, the 'do ut des' (the gift, that is, 'I give so that you give') and the 'unus pro toto' (the sacrifice, that is, the 'one instead of all') of the Ancient Romans brutally adds up in the slayed emissary who unites what is social into a coalition. *At the same time*, this is Christianity and anti-Semitism.

Therefore, in a dreadful way, it is the people who had shouted 'To death!' who were subjected to the cry 'To death!' that determined the fate of the West, the Occident.

Sometimes the stars rising in the night
    flee the earth,
      moving away from our fear.

The Storming of Brisach

During the assault, near the bridge, a horse, struck by a musket shot, collapsed. Just as soon, to the surprise of all the cavalry horsemen who were fighting, men and women as skinny as skeletons surged froth from the ditches, despite the peril, the cannonballs, the grapeshot, the battle. They were so famished that they ate the horse raw, each one carving it up with his knife. They all cleared off after devouring with their teeth the horse, still alive and fuming, and leaving behind the bloody bones in the snow. (The Storming of Brisach, 1640.)

*

Jack London wrote all his novels based on the fundamental human experience of being afraid of being eaten.

Wild beasts consider human beings to be comestible. We apparently form a species which, if it is not *sublime*, is in any case *succulent*.

In the eyes of wild animals, that is, in the eyes of the ancient gods, human beings are regarded as being delicious.

Societies are always conceived by London's heroes (whether they be dogs, wolves, or human beings) as packs of the dead.

Placed on branches, Sade's partners, male and female, seemed exquisite to the eagles of the Black Forest below Baden.

Naturalists report that, in a pack of canidae, the place in the hierarchy is never permanently acquired. The acceptance of the domination of the strongest members founds the group more than subservience or taming. For dogs, like wolves, servitude is spontaneous, restless, excited, if not happy, as in all regimes of terror.

CHAPTER 58

The Horde of Carrion Eaters

It seems that the lineage of human beings appeared on earth neither only once, in time, nor in a single place. Possibilities made trial runs, emerged in reality, were lost in reality. Other possibilities relayed them. The contingency of each individual is also that of all the species. The coexistence of different types of pre-human animals lasted for thousands of years. The lineage Homo dominated at a late period the double chance of survivals and coituses. As prey more and more naked become more and more predatory, not at all out of instinct, out of imitation, out of auto-domestication, human beings who were less and less 'Homo' progressed into the world. The progression was so slow that it can seem quick to the sedentary people we have become: about fifty kilometres by generation. Man covered the earth like a bad, very slow nit. He is the only animal who carries objects, who brings back home all kinds of meats, berries, wild game, fish, birds, brings back words and adventures to the hearth of mothers and the ears of little children, wives, daughters, the elderly—this is why the journey, which repeated itself in regurgitations, regressions, reports and gossip, narratives, significant or recurrent dreams, was slow.

As the carrier of his hunting spoils, the human being is also the carrier of his 'experience': he carries the linguistic tale that he never stops telling of his being put into the peril of dying.

Such is the secret meaning of the word ex-perience: he who comes out of perishing.

＊

What is a man? A stick for killing, an old sack for bringing back what has been killed (a kind of skin bag), a tongue for reporting—on the putting to death of that which has died—to the survivor (to the eater of that which is dead).

In the language of the Ik people, *Abang-Anaze* means *Ancestor of the Ancients*. In the myth, the Ancestor of the Ancients says:

'God has given to human beings a stick and hunger.'

A stick is called *nakut* and god is called *didigwari*: the withdrawn, the lost, the inaccessible.

There is no god, there is only the lost (what has been devoured).

Using language means praying to Lost.

Every meal, once, twice, three times per day, shares the return of that which has been killed, beneath the incisors and the canines—chews it, deforms it, ingests it, builds itself out of death.

Then anything that has been killed is lost in the darkness of the body, even as each body is itself a sack that has come out of an older sack.

*

Two million years ago, our ancestors hunted only animals that had the size of their hands. A million years ago, our ancestors would hunt together, in groups, animals bigger than themselves. We are grass eaters who have added to ourselves platters of great flesh-eating feasting that we called hunting, then sacrifice, then war. Hunting bands were made up of some twenty men. The tribes or the dialects brought together some twenty bands.

These linguistic societies count in twos: hunting then feasting. Head-on death, then hierarchical sharing.

Silence, then bringing back and reporting on it.

Dissociation, then association.

A group of murderers, then a marriage of females.

The basic battue is natural, sexual; it has a double base; this division worsens, indurates, then replicates itself in mores as in languages. If I define hunters as the 'predators of predation', I obtain the definition of human sublimation: violent death imitated (the putting to death used by the flesh-eaters was imitated by berry pickers, flint gatherers, parasites of dead prey, swallowers of the lost).

*

At first, human beings, holding their stick, *are* still the milieu walking within Presence. They never think of tomorrow. They are too famished. The Erstwhile always surges forth in their bonding soul, then in their body ingesting death now more ancient than they are.

In a second period, tomorrow and the Neolithic era emerge. The milieu tears apart into earth and world. The idea of 'tomorrow' (the idea of another day that will come after this day) arises towards ~10,000. The year is invented in its seasons and granaries. Thereafter, the next living year is *sown* in the inhumation of seeds that have been preserved from the dead year. For the Palaeolithic people, the environment (Being) is the *subject* of the band-family. Towards ~10,000, man dissociates himself from the other predators and becomes the subject facing that which is: the 'étant' (the other species). A link is woven between the human pack, logos, the past, genealogy. Agriculture consists of burying the most beautiful fruit from the past year. Burying the lost. The same thing with human beings in tombs. The same thing with the animals that they domesticate. One sacrifices (one *loses*) the most vigorous and the most beautiful of the band to offer it in *return*. One pushes the kouros into the Tyrrhenian sea. Abraham the Father pulls back the hair of his son Isaac to uncover his throat. The flint knife is raised over the best of one's self. Cybele hugs her dead son in her arms. Agave tears apart her son—the king Pentheus—and devours him alive on the Mont Cithaeron. Even unique gods give themselves over to death through the persona of their son.

*

Before the origin, human beings were merged with animals. They belonged to them. They were on their side. Then they became animals who donned the habits of all the animal species to speak to them by using decoys of all kinds, whistling, singing, dancing, mimicking, masking all the species. The first human specialization consisted of the shamans who, remembering that they had formerly been animals, persisted in journeying near the big animals of the originary hunting of quarry. They taught hunters the words of the other animals, their little melodies, their joys, their signs, their steps, their tricks, their customs, their stories, their thefts, their abductions, their hunts.

Everything indicated everywhere a murder.

This murder cannot be found because human guilt spontaneously seeks, behind a murder, a man put to death.

Murders of fathers are indeed at stake, but not of a human parricide.

The murder in question is the one learnt from the flesh-eaters and turned back against them.

The inhibitions of cruelty 'de-siderate' into humanity.

Disciples who exterminated their masters.

The intense cynegetic guilt of hunting societies is simple to formulate. The terror that humanity experiences is that the wild animals will come back against the hunters during a terrible hunt in the other direction.

Thus the universal invention of hell is merely the magnification of the big wide open mouth of a wild animal above the naked, defenceless body of each human being.

CHAPTER 59

On the Way Back

Telling a tale, Claude Lévi-Strauss once asserted, *is 'conte redire', 'tale retell'*, to tell the tale twice. Contradict means that which takes the path in the opposite direction. But the path in the opposite direction is the way back. The heart of what human beings dream, the 'rêvée', is the hunt in the opposite direction that pursues the day before. Thinking is devoted to the past. First, thinking hallucinates in the what is dreamt, the 'rêvée', and orientates the day that follows by the day that precedes, then it revives by means of nomination and signifies the world. Every myth is a third party that groups together one of the poles by opposing it to the other pole that the structure of language creates for it. Every myth opposes everything. Simply, its discourse goes in the opposite direction once the myth, after surviving the death scene, brings back the wild game. There is no myth that can be taken alive; there is no hunt that can be narrated *while* the predator kills his prey; there is never a tale in the present tense. The predator is the survivor of the tale, *in the past tense*, of what he has experienced (in the *afterwards* of the predation). Only the effectuation of death indicates, on the one hand, he who was the predator and, on the other

163

hand, he who was the prey. The predator is surprised to be victorious and alive. The prey, well beyond surprise, in the excess of surprise, is overturned into death.

*

Com-prehend means to take, with several others. Yet predation with several people is a pack. In consequence, if comprehending is never anything but killing, if perceiving is never anything but differentiating silhouettes that frighten, every praedatio is a transport of death, every narrator is a revenant from the world of the dead, every narration imposes a grammar of the past (is a return which can express the going forth only because the re-turn has taken place). Re-turn like the re-gard, 'the looking back', of the fawn at the bird. Like the re-gard of the bison at the excrement. Like the re-gard of the hunter at the dead being. Like the re-gard of Orpheus at Eurydice. Even as the bee in the hive says, by dancing in front of all the bees in the hive, the corolla and the flower and the bush and the direction and the distance and the way. Even as the shaman travels, and like his odos-bird, upon its return to this world, alighting on the top of his stick, re-tells the trip in the second world that is the third realm. Way resaying the way. Sky that must go back across itself every year according to the time indicated by the duration of its voyage. Every myth prophesies the advent that has taken place. The hunter telling of his hunt begins with a beginning of death, which leads him to the now-aliveness restored by death. The narrator who hides behind the narration is the act inventing the past to reactivate the passage of the passer-by to the past. Violent death constitutes the depth. Even as the dream hallucinates what has disappeared, been ingested, is absent, even as the word refers to a thing that is no longer, the tale is never in the indicative (is never contemporary to the action that it brings back, re-ports on, along with the prey that it brings back) and never has its sources in the language that narrates it. This is the secret of translations. Translations between homogeneous or foreign or allogeneous languages are possible because the act of trans-lation, carrying across, comes first. The future predator sets out in quest of the prey that is other, after the fashion of the language that is other. Trans-latio, trans-port, meta-phora, trans-fer (death, ingestion, digestion, ejection)—the myth transports its contents like a hunter who carries on his shoulder a 'brought-back', a 're-ported', that is linked to a murder anterior to his own return, for it is the murder of what is hunted that permits his return towards the group that is going to cut up the body, distribute the pieces, feast at last. In Chinese, the character signifying man is an arrow. The arrow of time and the arrow of predation are synchronous, beginning with the death that they have inflicted formerly and, at the same time, suddenly on the other being.

CHAPTER 60

Vultur

The first man given a figurative representation in the General History of human beings has the head of a raptor and he is falling backwards into death.

Upright at his feet is the soul stick gripped by the claws of the raptor.

The Mazdaistic Dakhmas refer to the celestial funerals or sky burials which are the most ancient usages of the dead because they preceded human beings until the times of dinosaurs and dragons, of which birds of prey are the small derivative celestial creatures.

This separation between the living and the dead is done in nature by the beaks of birds between the earth and the sky.

Surviving men would hang the corpses of their close ones in the branches of trees; they would expose them on mountain peaks; they would place them atop stone towers. Either they would leave them to the disposal of birds, which would separate the flesh from the bones, or the corpses would be stolen by birds and winged off into the sublime emptiness of the air.

The time-stick characteristic of the ancient Japanese and Siberian peoples is a crow-stick. It's the black bird that is found with the first 'man' imago and even on his face. The death-bearing crow, beginning with the brain, became a soul-carrier who transported all the way to the images constellating the black depths of the sky. In the most beautiful piece of writing in the world, Zhuang Zhou asked that his body be placed on the branches of a tree. Once the decarnalization had been accomplished in a few hours, the still-connected bones would remain. Then the cultural funeral, strictly speaking, began.

It was in 1960 that the Shah prohibited, over all the territory of Iran, the sky burials of human beings in towers of silence.

*

Kipling belonged to a family of bell-founders who lived in Bombay. He was born in the shadow of a tower of silence. The towers of Bombay were high towers with terraces on which were placed the corpses of men, on steps, so that the birds would clean them. The birds transported the devoured souls as far as possible from the earth (where human beings live) and very near the sky (where the gods are imagined as birds that are bigger and more invisible than the other birds in their midst). The birds tore the fate of human beings from the eschatological stain of rotting. They removed them from the predation of the big mammals. Only the beings of the sky transferred the 'souls' into the blue where the sky becomes infinite. They recycled the breaths of respiration in the winds that pushed the clouds above the valleys and the mounts of the earth. They projected the sparks of life into the fire of the sun.

*

One day, when the little Kipling boy was playing in the garden, a vulture let go of a child's hand that fell near him.

Kipling reports that he still felt fright as he jotted down this memory that came back to him from early childhood.

Raptors are our tombs.

They are the genuine Sirens.

They begin with the eye.

Once the eye is consumed, their beaks and neck plunge into the socket. Here is the order with which they proceed: first and foremost, they eat vision. Then they devour thoughts. Finally, it is the soft, tepid, throbbing entrails of our passions. It is only later that the question is raised about the flesh and the more substantial muscles that mammals and also ourselves, the human beings, quarrel over with the birds.

This sharing is the sacrifice.

The hair, the bones, the teeth, the feathers and the furs find no animals, in none of the three worlds, to dispose of them.

We were this: we get dressed.

This meant nourishing the hope to share their company.

Of what animal were we not the animal?

Getting dressed meant remembering them. They were our headgear, our cache-sexes, our scarves, our soles, our coats, our flutes, our whistles, our pair of dice, our knives, belts, bracelets, marvellous necklaces below the face, ear-rings around the face, crowns above the face.

*

Vultur (from which we have made the vulture) referred to the bid that devoured the face (*vultus*) of the dead.

Vultur goes back to *vellere*: to tear away by pulling.

*

The bearded vulture is a bird whose size seems immense to the human being over whom it flies. Its wingspan is two and a half metres. It extracts the marrow from the smallest bones by using its sharp tongue. It breaks the biggest bones by letting them drop on rocks.

Aeschylus died in ~450. A bearded vulture let a tortoise drop on the bald head of the first Tragic Author of Greece.

Pliny wrote: A bearded vulture killed Aeschylus. (Pliny the Elder suggests that the bird had taken the naked skull of the great Tragic Author for a rock and had reckoned on disconcerting its prey.)

*

A raptor's attack rarely lasts more than ten seconds.

The rapidity was preceded by the rapacity.

Two times are clearly articulated in the world that has been raised on earth: waiting while turning in a circle, suddenly rushing in a line.

The raptor is the difference between slowness and rapidity turned into an animal. The difference between duration and event became the difference between circulus and linea. The imitation of the raptor was the invention of the throwing stick, which added force to the line. Then the throwing stick dreamt of its return in the boomerang. Finally, the stick culminated in the miraculous invention of the arrow taking support from the space carrying it.

*

Vultures were the gods of men at a time when we were still but carrion eaters carrioning near black crows, hobbling like them when they walk on dry mud.

Vultures were the dogs of gods at a time when wolves had not yet become the dogs of men. (For we had so many masters. One day, the societies of wolves from eastern Asia approached men. Little by little, the wolves led the men to collaborate with their hunts and taught them their tricks of encirclement and harassment.)

*

The *Vultur*, as it soars, constitutes the depth of reading.

Not only do vultures trace out the first line, they also mark, above the faces of men, the first point.

Men would follow their flight into the sky; men would go all the way to the point that the raptors indicated by their soaring. At the very plumb line where they were turning in a circle in the sky, men would find remains (vestigia, reliquiae) of a dead beast that the wild animals had already killed or that an accident had thrown down on the earth; that the vultures had already enucleated, excerebrated, eviscerated. Once men had arrived on the spot, they quarrelled over the beast and defended it against the other hyenas, lionesses, tigers, rats, wolves and foxes that gathered there as they still gather in fables left over from that time.

This circle, on the plumb line of this point, forms the first sign.

*

Raptors, flesh-eaters, carrion eaters: the 'having stolen', the 'having bounded', the 'having passed by'.

There is a pre-sacrifice to the sacrifice.

There is a pre-hierarchy to the hierarchy.

The abandonment of carrion eating raised a problem for the most ancient human beings when they moved on to active hunting—which was not an instinct in them, but rather mere flesh-eating activity mimicked with much care and fear. In myths, tales, annals, legends, the call of the vulture's daughters is the call of the past. This is why the Sirens sing the Erstwhile and—when they sing the Erstwhile—they say in Greek: 'Deuro.' In Latin: 'Hic.' In French: 'Ici.' It is the 'here' of the carrion that the first of the 'signs' refers to, beginning with the sky sung by the raptors.

Where death is on the plumb line is where it comes at just the right time.

The most ancient men would follow the carrion eaters in the diurnal sky—even as the three wise men would keep their eyes fixed on a star which moved in the nocturnal sky and guided their steps, which orientated the slow progression, in the direction of the orient, of the camels of their caravan.

By indicating the fallen prey, the raptors signalled the first community feast to the flesh-eaters.

These are the first great circles in the site that brings men together beginning with the point that they project vertically from the sky to the earth. These are the first temples, even before their walls rise along the plumb line of the site that they divide up by projecting it on the earthly space. These are the first celestial dances before those, so impassive, of the stars day and night during a year's time, and of those however weightier and more passionate dances, in their image, of human beings hailing their apparitions above them.

Ever higher a semiophore-animal representing the invisible ones, an indication of the appealing cadavers, the witness of the dead, the mark of the ancestors, the augur of gods.

An invisible representative of the Anteriors to the Scene anterior to every human being.

A Creator in the Genesis.

The rex-augur is the sky carver. With his lituus, he draws from right to left (from east to west) the page over which the vultures will fly. This pagina is called a templum (this land is called a rectangle). Romulus is the king-sooth-sayer who interprets omens. Every hero with a split person-ality is a shaman who travels and joins his auxiliary. The bird and the bird carrier walk in pairs.

The Ik people say: Vultures and Human Beings are alike.

The Romans said: Either vultures or wolves. These were their gods.

Three aces in Rome, in a dice game, formed the sign of the Underworld. This toss of the dice was called *Canes aut Vulturii* (Dogs and Vultures).

*

In Latin, 'to speculate' means to watch from the heights of a place for any sign of death in order to dive down on it like a carrion eater.

In the depths of space, this lookout that goes round in circles, that waits for what it desires—such is the sun, which goes from east to west, grandfather of the vision that contemplates it.

In the depths of time, behind the language that organizes it, is positioned this state of animal alertness, of patient lying-in-awaitness that remains silent and speculates.

Then once again, as *en archè*, as *a principio*, as *ja-a-dis* ('erstwhile', 'already there was a day'), time absorbs space and swallows up within it he who is lying in wait.

*

A goddess dated ~5000 was shattered when she was conveyed on a hand truck into the marvellous Alexandria National Museum. The two wheels of the hand truck were screeching on the waxed wooden floor. Suddenly there is a noise of balls falling: the museum floor is strewn with beaks. The clay breasts of the goddess were full of vulture beaks.

CHAPTER 61

Héraklès in the Desert

When Héraklès reached Egypt, the hero discovered that he was a victim. The man who was wandering over the sand dunes, watched by eagles, spotted by lions, was no hero: he was a prey.

We have no need to postulate that there is a fundamental aggressiveness in us.

Being hunted by animals and devoured by them forms an originary, long-lasting traumatism, not only before prehistory but also during prehistory, with a long sedimentation in a brain which, little by little, by dint of eating flesh, increases in size.

The sacralization of violence finds its source in the terror inspired by the famished wild animal—tenacious, obsessed, untameable, unappeasable, insatiable, uncompromising—which lies in wait for us as his next meal.

The historical period begins when human beings, having exterminated the big beasts of prey, supplanting little by little in quantity the wild animals that they had decimated, penning them up in the paradises of temples, domesticating the animals that submitted to their domination in pens, had more to fear from each other than from the species that had taught them beauty, civilization, sly tricks, terror.

CHAPTER 62

Grimm the Elder wrote: Three languages share the world. What dogs bark. What birds sing. What frogs croak.

In what dogs bark, it must be understood that the main joy of society is war. Because what dogs bark is the enemy.

In what birds sing, it must be understood that the first period of the hominids consisted of carrion feasting, which they had learnt from the vultures. Because what birds sing is death.

In what frogs croak at night, in the summer heat, in ponds scattered among the thickets of the limestone plateaus or in the bushes of the heaths, it must be understood that, when hunger has been assuaged, the body receives its recompense in the voluptuousness by which it reproduces its silhouette.

What frogs croak during the nights is the sexual desire rising in their bodies once their appetite is satisfied. With their lips still bloody from the dead prey, the souls dream of their return to life in the coming sleep.

CHAPTER 63

Lün's Meals

The name of Freud's last chow-chow was Lün. Freud knew that he had to make the decision to kill himself when his dog refused to come close to him because he smelt so much of death. His mouth stank of the cancer devouring him. The dog began to flee from the odour given off by the mouth of the man whom he loved. It was 1 September, the day when Germany invaded Poland. Freud committed suicide, with the help of Doctor Max Schur. The doctor then gave him three shots of morphine. After Freud's burial, Anna Freud and Paula Fichtl treated the dog of death like a genuine divinity. Every day, at the end of breakfast, the first thing that the two women did was to put together *Lün's meals*.

CHAPTER 64

Mr and Mrs Blois of Artigues

On 1 February 1959, Mr and Mrs Blois went to the town hall and asked for the authorization to bury their dog Félix—which had been, to tell the truth, a dog as happy as it was marvellous—in the family vault. The mayor of Artigues told them to do as they wished. So Mr and Mrs Blois placed their dog in the tomb, as they had desired to do. The inhabitants of the town of Artigues were outraged. They lodged a complaint, feeling that it was an insult to the dignity of their dead ones to be next to the grave of a dog. Having refused to disinter Félix, Mr and Mrs Blois were summoned to the Libourne Police Court. The Council of State decreed that the mayor had acted without legal authority by authorizing the inhumation of a dog in a cemetery. Celtic cemeteries, which regional archaeological societies disinter every time a tollway is built, bring to light human beings, horses, chariots, swords, lances, shields, dogs, princesses.

*

In the Roman Underworld, a dog stands on the threshold.

There is a past that has never been present.

An anterior realm emerges as such around each sign.

There is only one scene that has never been visible to us and that concerns us more than anything.

It is our body.

The anterior scene is there where we are, we of whom the flesh and the face are the only vestiges.

The moment of the first person does not exist; it is always another person, two other people, a wound, an Outside, a childhood, a persecution that takes its place.

The empty place of the first person, which is only a banging door, must be hidden in the world.

*

What is power? The possibility possessed by a society or a State, at any moment, to turn back an individual at the border by declaring him to be non-human, non-national, non-subjective, tearing his face from him at the same time as his biography, flinging them into death or emptiness.

*

Cave canem.

Caute.

Beware.

Beware of the dog that threatens everywhere.

Beware twice, that is, look twice ('re-garde'), that is, be afraid.

*

'Mistrust' was the name of the 'March of Naked Monks' during the 1960s, in Japan. It was also called the 'Hiroshima-Auschwitz Peace March'.

*

Stevenson wrote: He, I say—I cannot say I. Nothing lived in him but fear.

Nothing lives in one's depths but the distress of birth abandoning one helplessly to screaming hunger, that is, to the empty body.

He, is God.

So they asked:

'Ubi, Domine?'

'Where, Lord?'

And God—the Unnameable, the Unsayable—replied to them:

'Where the vultures will gather.'

God Himself says in the Bible: The sign (signum) is there where eagles gather (congreagabuntur aquilae).

*

What is the heart of self? Emptiness. The emptiness of hunger. The emptiness that is emptied out by hunger in the depths of self gathers the self after the fashion of a pocket that envelops emptiness.

The demand that I address to he whom I am not pre-supposes the emptiness, in the depths of myself, which makes my place.

A dog barks at the moon.

A dog barks, facing the carrion whose form decomposes little by little until it vanishes in the emptiness of the sky.

Irresistible celestial carrion in which a vegetarian monkey is going to be interested by dint of dying of emptiness, in his hunger.

A simiomorph becomes the hunting companion of wolves, jackals, coyotes, hyenas, dogs.

He is won over not to the humanity within him but to being a predator of the predators.

He is won over by watching the *wolf that devours the moon piece by piece in the night sky while howling.*

*

Stevenson: I kill the god whom I hide (hyde). Laws formulate, in regard to the human heart, a kind of vain self-criticism that no society observes, that private individuals damage, that criminals trample. The tables of the law, the lists of prohibited acts, the codes of customs, the volumes of good manners, the declarations on the rights of man, of woman, of the child, of minorities, of the dead ones of each family in the Artigues Cemetery, the right ways to hold one's knife and fork at the table, roam between forms of sarcasm and dreaming.

*

In order to understand what sacrifice is, one must have seen the simple, slow, serious and silent eating of spoils in nature. For example, a group of Rüppel's vultures fight over the carcass of a putrefied cow: the strongest predators forcefully use their beaks, claws, hooves, wings, horns, incisors or antlers to push away the other animals which are as famished as they are and which are obliged to wait until the first ones are full. Sharing the prey is a hierarchy in time; a temporization; the lion kills; the eagle signals; the hyena or the man comes running.

I copy down Jacques Lacan's sentence: 'Speech can play the role of the carrion very well. In all cases, speech is not more unappetizing.'

The work of de Sade is the extraordinary crumb of the originary spoils.

*

Civilization and its Discontents is dated 1930. *Why War?* is dated 1933. Psychoanalysis brings no solution to the disorder of the world, because there is no solution to the disorder of the world. Endless war. The primitive scene that makes up the heart of the doctrine is the sexually excited naked father and the naked mother who is penetrated by him and moaning because of his thrusts. The nucleus thus puts forth three faces: the primitive scene, Oedipus, the sex drive of death. But it is the same face. This trio makes one. The son kills the father who begets him. Eros chains up that which, inside Eros, Thanatos unchains. The sex drive of death defines nothing else than Sadism. The inner world is as much in war as the outer world can be, in front of us.

CHAPTER 65

Hunger is at the source of the most haunting metamorphosis of bodies. A body eats another body. This is the secret exchange of life. It is the secret centre of the metamorphosis of beings. Ovid himself gives a justification for this in line 187 of the seventh book of *The Metamorphoses*: for fates (the fata, the fairies) do not allow Ceres and Hunger to ever meet. They don't like each other. They never go together (co-ire).

Ovid shows Hunger living on Mount Caucasus.

Hunger is an image of a woman: completely skinny, almost transparent. She wanders over an unreachable land swept by snow-bearing winds. She is shaggy-haired, her eyes are sunken, her lips are blue with cold, her bones poke out from skin that has become translucent by dint of her thinness. When the sun rises, she can be seen, on all fours, on a stony field, already in the process of tearing out, with her canines, the few blades of grass that she has managed to find.

The two empty pockets of her breasts seem to hang directly from the rack of her spine.

Suddenly she raises her head, she arches her head towards the sky, she raises her eyes into the air, she opens her mouth, she spits out a little mist, she moves her jaws, she wears out her teeth on her teeth.

She devours the impalpable air surrounding her and, filling herself with air, increases the emptiness hollowing her out.

Desubjectivation is the self fallen back to the state of a dying body.

Desubjectivation was passionately sought out during the dehumanization of the twentieth century.

Originary desubjectivation occurs when one is recognized by another animal as a piece of meat. This is what Géricault meditated upon for a year, closing himself up in his studio, increasing the number of preparatory sketches, charcoal and chalk drawings, gouaches, water-colours, as well as the fragmentary, indeed prodigious oil paintings of the *Raft of the Medusa*. What Géricault was seeking at night in his studio was more archaic than sacrifice. Fascination is the heart of specifically human shame. To be acknowledged as a desiring animal by a clothed human being who speaks and gives orders sinks the soul into shame. Such is the scene that fascinates masochists prior to all rituals. This scene overwhelms them with an originary joy. It is the heart of all myths. It is the predator who has again become prey.

CHAPTER 66

War

One should look in printing-shop type cases to find the thickest capital letters and spread red ink over them so that the most important things that need to be said about the history of human beings on the earth will never be omitted.

Hunting is exciting but war is full of passion. War breaks limits. War opens the souls of men to another psychic state (a state more ancient even than originary, without hierarchy, without family, without cleanliness, without a time schedule). War is the soul of everyone on the alert, with age groups now showing solidarity with each other as they impatiently await the next moment, the body sunk into an anguish mixed with fever, time having become unanimous in the event that can be shared by anyone in ever-new 'news' whose newness is incessantly renewed. It is the tocsin. It is awakening with a start, hours having become substantial, History significant. In war, every day cannot only be narrated but also every day *becomes* the narrator. The experience that assails there is a 'to-be-told' that incessantly goes forward, from 'main headline' to 'main headline', from front page to front page, day after day, newspaper after newspaper, from event to event, from wave to wave, from sudden appearance to sudden appearance.

'To-be-told' is called legendum in Latin. Hunting and war are the founders of the 'to-be-told' of language, and project time into legend. Every national language is provided with its legend by war. This is what is called the History of Peoples, where every people writes down only a fallacious history in 'its' language. And this generic history, beneath the Histories of the various peoples, is always a history of inter-human war that takes on the form of a tale of hunting animals. It is a regressive tale. Dying in war is the 'cultural' death par excellence. The first human figurative representation is a dying hunter. Beginning with the Neolithic period, war founds social time. The considerable sacrifice of males to which war consents indicates epochs during centuries and dates new eras during millennia. One needs to put one's fingers in one's ears when hearing the hypocritical invectives that human beings have sometimes levelled against war; human beings were not subjected to war; they invented it; and human beings invented war because they loved it; because they loved this exceptional state extending everywhere; because they loved this kind of time suddenly broken off from other kinds of time; because they adored the temporal ecstasy, the force that was spread, reinforced, reinforcing, streaming, colourful, excited, exciting, fascinating, invigorating. War is the human feast par excellence. It is the long holiday from life that is normal, harassed, divided, unhappy, obedient, serf-like, constrained, familial, reproductive, amorous.

*

War is a bacchanalian orgy, a leave from reproduction.

It is Caesar's famous statement: War is horrible from up close; it is beautiful only in its midst.

Fighting is one of the most ancient animal joys. A pre-human euphoria bears along all the species. The ancient word virtus, with the two traits that defined it (momentum of sap, laugh of death), is the pleasure that can be taken in life to show one's teeth in order to show one's desire to eat, to rise up in combat, to establish oneself by means of bold-ness and cruelty.

*

Homer shows Achilles (in *The Iliad* I, 491) as immobile, his heart *wasting away* while he remains without fighting. *Polemos* torments him. He stands next to the black ship held by the props on the sandy shore. He is gloomy, longing so much for *the war cry and the battle*.

*

Every night, in a dream that is different each time, for the last eight years of his life, that is, for 2920 times during 2920 nights, an aged Marcus Claudius Marcellus, with his hair ever whiter, faced Hannibal *in a pitched battle behind a palisade*.

*

Never omit the pleasure of fighting in regard to the cause of wars.

And never omit hunger: the strange viscosity of social functioning, its almost seasonal burdensomeness and its daily circularity are originary. The oral waiting of hunger every day, the daily anal thrust, the urinary pruritus, the nightly erection and the nychthemeral rhythm of sleep form the same thrust.

Like a tide.

The Stoics said: A single drive (in Greek a single orexis, in Latin a unique impetus) carries the world as if it were a whole—and everyone hides in order to do what everyone does.

Poor anal joy defecating out of oneself the other devoured death and in that way become oneself. Cyclic intimate stench.

Poor annual poles of cold and heat. Mountain and sea. Human society is a big animal with odd habits that are tedious, vulgar, repetitive, circular and cruel, and that *are entertained only by only war*.

*

À la guerre comme à la guerre! (In war, as in war. We'll just have to make the best of things.) Every tautology indicates what is originary. In hunting, as in hunting. In death, as in death, etc.

One needs to see every morning the cat waiting in front of the kitchen door, watching it open, rising proudly, putting out its paws in the moist grass and leaving the calm and warmth of the house, abandoning the garden for the dawn mist over the little dry fork of the river.

It's Montaigne who wrote this other terrible sentence: Hunting without killing is like loving without sexual pleasure.

*

On Christmas eve in 1793, on 24 December, Mallarmé (Stéphane Mallarmé's great uncle), read to the Convention the report made by General Westermann, who had fought victoriously the evening before in Savenay: 'Vendée no longer exists. It has died under our free sabre. I have crushed children under the hooves of the horses. I have massacred all the women brigands who will no longer give birth to brigands. I have not a single prisoner to reproach myself for. Bread must be kept for the Revolutionaries.'

*

With every declaration of war, social temporality again becomes like a wild beast that stops all of a sudden, that curls up, that pulls back at full speed on its muscles before leaping, in order to leap, before once again attempting a sortie on the earth.

Time that attempts a sortie from time into death that is no longer natural, but given.

CHAPTER 67

D'Annunzio

The Birth of Tragedy was written in the joy of the victory over France. The preface, dated 1871, evokes the euphoria of Germany, which has become an Empire, and associates this to the triumph ultimately enjoyed by Wagner's music. Nietzsche dies in Weimar in 1900. Gabriele d'Annunzio understood Nietzsche exactly as his sister Elisabeth had interpreted him. Not only did D'Annunzio introduce Nietzsche's thought into Italy, he also takes himself for Wagner: he writes a new kind of theatrical play, he invents a new 'ceremony'. 'War', he declares, is the 'total social feast'. Beginning in 1909, D'Annunzio calls for a new world war to overturn old Europe. Marinetti follows him, in the *Second Manifesto of Futurism*, in 1911: 'War is the only hygiene in the world.' In 1913, D'Annunzio asserts: 'We breathe who knows what fragrance of a miracle in which alternate, in a story crossed by flashes of lightning, truth and dream, current life, and the most remote fable.' The Armistice takes place on 11 November 1918 in Rethondes. On 18 May 1919, D'Annunzio receives the gold medal of military merit. On 23 June, Mussolini meets him. The same day, the King of Italy explains to D'Annunzio that he will not modify the 'statuto' (the Italian institutions). On 1 July,

D'Annunzio publishes 'Disobbedisco' ('I Disobey') in *L'Idea Nazionale*. On 11 September, at 1.30 p.m., D'Annunzio, having donned a lieutenant-colonel's uniform, takes a seat aboard the motorboat that conducts him to San Giuliano Point. On the 12th, at high noon, D'Annunzio, in charge of 2,200 men, enters Fiume, announces its annexation and settles in the Europa Hotel. The Lega di Fiume intends to gather into a 'compact fasces' all the 'peoples and races wronged by the Versailles Conference'.

*

In 1925, on Lake Garda, B. Mussolini offers to G. D'Annunzio a 'hydroplane so that he can stroll above the water'.

CHAPTER 68

Long ago, a man loved war but he was restive with respect to any kind of power; he would disobey any party whatsoever until he ended up reuniting with his astonishing first name, which was that of a natal distress. Agrippa d'Aubigné is individualism that is samurai-like, bloody, unconventional, banned, exiled, censured. In 1620, his *Universal History* was burnt in public. Writing does not mean only integration, legitimation, recognition, academization in palaces, glory in posterity. For Agrippa d'Aubigné, writing implied a religious anachoresis as opposed to the common religion, the desert as opposed to towns, vengeance for his executed family members, faithfulness to the defeated, and adventure, oblivion. He is a man of letters conceived of as the spokesman for the dead, swallowed up by the silence before languages. D'Aubigné seems to be a sixteenth-century writer whereas he wrote during the reign of Louis XIII, even as Stendhal appeared to be, in Flaubert's eyes, an eighteenth-century novelist transported into the reign of Charles X and the Ministry of Joseph de Villèle.

*

At Archiac, where he had to leave the front three times because the horses that he was riding died, three times, under him, Agrippa the Unsaddled came back three times on a new horse to enjoy the pleasure of shedding blood *a little more*. Everywhere, he writes, *he made detours* to kill because he loved fighting so much. More than pitched battles, he loved hand-to-hand combat, guerrilla warfare, loading his pistol, the *fifteen-horse skirmishes*.

*

The history of France opens with Rauchingue, in the sixth century, the warrior who 'exulted' in carnage. The history of France 'exulted' once again with de Sade, at the end of the eighteenth century. Then it was 'overwhelmed' with joy in the Revolution of the French, before it was finally 'overturned', at the end of the Great Terror, and crushed during the Empire.

The terrible expression *exultation in cruelty* already appears in Gregory of Tour's *Chronicles*.

Rauchingue loved night. A millennium before Caravaggio, Zurbarán, Valentino and Georges de La Tour, Rauchingue devoted all his joys to the night. He had instituted a 'night service' that consisted of twelve torch-bearers. At the beginning of the feast, he would designate one of the servants to carry a flaming wax torch in front of him, force him to snuff it out on his naked leg, then he would have the torch lit again from the flame of the nearest torch and begin again until the leg was completely black.

Like Caravaggio, Zurbarán, Valentino and Georges de La Tour, Rauchingue loved the night and the silence of this game of light and nakedness.

Every evening, when the servant screamed, if he could not hold back a moan, if his face showed him wrenching from pain, Rauchingue would lift his 'scramaseax' and behead him.

Even in the old word scramaseax, sex remains as a suffix.

The Bishop Gregory of Tours (who knew Rauchingue and who apparently also did not flinch during those nightly services that he attended as the Bishop of Tours) writes that one had to see, to observe, during the entire nightly feast the child tortured by his own light *in* his own light, which he held in a hand that mustn't tremble near his face.

Then the bishop writes, precisely, that to see the hapless fellow who sought to remain impassive and who let tears fall in silence along his cheeks made Rauchingus 'exult with great joy' (*magna laetitia exultaret*).

*

Tiresias says that the theatre is reserved for terrible knowledge. The son kills his father (Oedipus, Hamlet), the mother kills her child (Medea, Agave), women tear apart their lovers, men kill their god. The Passion of Jesus is the last lusus, the last Roman game of the ancient world, the last ludibrium of the ancient Etruscans. At the end, the father kills the son. In the Gospels, Abraham really kills Isaac. This kind of nocturnal, totally nocturnal Nô play, stages a king who is mocked, naked, crowned with thorns, put to death like a slave.

The scene occurs at night, takes place in two phases. At the top of the mount, around a cross that has been raised in the stormy night and lit by a flash of lightning. Subsequently, in a courtyard engulfed by night, sunk into the cold, near the red embers of a fire, before the cock crows, before dawn breaks.

The phantom appears twice: as a gardener in a garden, in front of a turned-over stone, in the morning at dawn. Then as a fellow traveller walking towards a village, halting at an inn, taking a seat at a table, breaking bread, in the evening twilight.

CHAPTER 69

Rocola and Torgahaut

The girl's name was Rocola. The young man's name was Torgahaut. They were both servants of Duke Rauchingue. Their youthfulness and beauty were extraordinary. They had reached the age of adolescence, but they were still children. They loved each other with so much force that they could conceal it from no one. This mutual attachment (*mutuo amore*) had already lasted two years. In 579, the rumour went around that the lord's intendant was going to separate them when spring came. They immediately became alarmed. Rocola said to Torgahaut:

'I fear for our love.'

Torgahaut said to Rocola:

'I fear for your life.'

'I am certain that we are going to be separated.'

'Now that you have expressed your worry, it has reached me.'

'Torgahaut, Torgahaut, I really fear for our love. We must flee.

Torgahaut replied to Rocola:

'Let's wait for the noumenia. We will flee when every-one has fallen asleep. By then the rooms of the castle will be steeped in the darkest night of the month.'

So they awaited the night of the new moon. After the feast, after the torch torture, when the room had been cleaned up again, everyone sunk into sleep, they fled from the estate into total darkness. They ran for several miles. They were still walking, by the end of the night. At dawn, at the hour of the first Mass, they entered a church that belonged to a monastery at which they asked for asylum. The door to the convent adjoining the nave of the church was opened for them. They asked to see the Father Abbot. As soon as the Father Abbot appeared, Rocola knelt, then lay down on the stone pavement, her face against the ground. Torgahaut got down on his knees, raised his hand towards the Father Abbot, implored him, avowed their love, explained the project that Rauchingue's intendant had conceived. He added that their love was so strong that nothing could separate them and that they would prefer dying.

'Dying? You speak of dying?'

The Father Abbot had Rocola confirm this threat, which was impious.

Rocola stood up on the stone floor of the church.

'Yes', she said, raising her arms. 'I love Torgahaut and only him, and will so forever.'

'What then would you intend to do if he were far from you?'

'I swear that I would kill myself forthwith if I were separated from Torgahaut.'

Once Rocola had pronounced this terrible oath, the monks withdrew. They conferred. They resolved to bless the union to avoid committing a sin that would deliver them to eternal flames.

The Father Abbot married them.

＊

When Rauchingue learnt that the two servants had married without his knowing, he mounted his horse. He went to the priests and demanded his two slaves. The Father Abbot replied:

'You know Church law. You know that you are not at liberty to take back your two servants unless you take an oath to maintain their sacred union, which they have contracted in front of our Lord. I remind you that our Lord, for us monks, dwells in heaven and holds all the powers in his hand. Finally, the law imposes upon you that you can in no way inflict corporal punishment on these two children once they have become man and wife in front of us.'

Listening to these words, Rauchingue at first remained stupefied.

Without moving, he was thinking.

Then he raised his hands onto the altar and took an oath by saying exactly:

'Numquam erunt a me separandi.'

This means: Never will they be separated by me. Once he had done this, he turned to the assembly of monks. In front of them, facing them, with his hands extended, he declared not only that Torgahaut and Rocola would never be separated by him, but, in addition, that he would take care that they always remained united.

The priest then sent for Torgahaut and Rocola, who had become man and wife. (Because they had become man and wife, they now lived outside of the monastery and its chastity.)

They entered, holding hands.

The two spouses were marvellously beautiful, clean, well-dressed, blushing with modesty when they came through the doorway.

But they began to tremble, like leaves when autumn appears, when they spotted their lord.

However, the duke imparted no reproach.

The Father Abbot repeated in front of them the oath that Rauchingue had made. Then he handed them over to their master.

*

Back on his estate, Rauchingue had Torgahaut and Rocola sit down next to him, on a bench, and had them drink pure wine, until their thirst was quenched, to celebrate their marriage; in front of them, he had one of his thick oak trees felled; he had its trunk hollowed out; he had a four-foot-deep hole dug in the ground of the clearing; he slid the hollowed-out tree in there, like a kind of boat. He had Rocola, who was weeping, taken and gently lain on her back and, afterwards, he threw down (*praecipit*) the unhappy Torgahaut, whom she loved, on top of her so he would face her. A board closed the narrow opening of the tree and swallowed up the two lovers in its shadow. The dirt that had been dug was tossed over them. The hole was filled and levelled. Then Rauchingue pronounced exactly the following words:

'Non frustravi juramentum meum ut non separarentur.'

This means: I have not failed to keep my oath: they will never be separated.

The Father Abbot learnt of this; he hurriedly arrived with his monks; he accused Rauchingue of having failed to keep his oath; Rauchingue argued that he had not betrayed his oath; he had not punished them; he had not killed them; he had not separated them; the Father Abbot admonished him at length and finally obtained his agreement to have the two young spouses—whose union he had blessed—dug back up. Unfortunately, it was too late; the servant man was alive when he was extricated from the earth, but the young woman, whose name was Rocola, was dead in his arms. Torgahaut was mourning her. He wiped off the dirt that had remained on his clothes. He said:

'I survived because I had my nose in the mouth of the woman I loved.'

He left with the Father Abbot. He became a monk. He never got over his love. All life long, he repeated: 'I survived because I had my nose in the mouth of the woman I loved.'

CHAPTER 70

Excitare

It is said that Vitellius, in Cremona, decided to see again, *forty days after the battle,* the killing ground because he had experienced so much good luck, felt so much happiness. He went onto the battlefield, surrounded by his guards. He progressed between the rotting cadavers of men and horses. He was by no means bothered by the putrid stench rising from the piled-up bodies. 'He chuckled to himself while recalling the beautiful blows that he had given, the heroes that he had disembowelled. He pronounced the name of the heads that he had decapitated while everything was covered with flies.'

*

On 22 January 1588, Henri IV wrote that the mere word 'battle', whenever he heard it, *virtuated* ('évertuait') his body. He said that he neither hated nor loved his enemies, but that he had to resign himself to their existence *because the battle came with them.* 'Battling', he wrote in his letters, consists of 'making a rage'.

The writer whom I preferred reading in the twentieth century was named 'Bataille'.

One day, in the numerous letters that have been preserved from his reign, King Henri IV confided to one Monsieur de Sainte-Colombe: 'I would hang myself for this pleasure.'

*

The definition of politics was given by Monsieur Jules Delahaye, at the National Assembly, during the session of 23 November 1892: 'It's the spoils, lying in broad daylight, of the wealth of citizens, poor people and people in need, protected by men whose mission is to protect it. What stands out in Jules Delahaye's definition is 'lying in broad daylight'.

*

Parisian students demonstrated during the first few days of July 1870. Every day, they left the Sorbonne, heading for the Boulevards. They were brandishing flags and banners. They were singing hilariously, taking up the tune of the 'Lampions' chanted in 1848: 'On to Berlin! On to Berlin!'

One needs to reread the newspapers from 1914. One must read the insane joy that grabbed hold of all the peoples of Europe at the idea of *going to war*.

*

'To excite' is not at first a sexual verb concerning the genitals of lovers seized with tumefaction, distension, erection, blushing, tremors.

'To be excited' was at first said of dogs. A pack of excited dogs indicates a group of dogs that has been sicced on the prey by means of screams and spears. This means pushing the famished auxiliaries towards the alter. To bring out the prey. To make it emerge. To make it surge forth.

Citation and excitation have the same lair, and the reader is the hunter.

To hunt down and to read are not distinguished as acts by the man of letters: in-citation of passages that the eyes read and excitation of fragments that his hand tears away from the books that he reads.

*

Spoils in Latin defines the *erotic desire for the torn prey*.

Every pack (*turba*), writes Ovid, is *cupidine praedae*.

A people defines the community inhabited by the 'Cupido of preys'.

This desire visits not only men but also dogs.

*

Tradition has preserved not only the names of all the dogs that devoured Acteon but also preserved the order in which the devouring of the prey took place. First, it was

Melanchaetes who, emerging behind Acteon, gave him the first bite in the back. Theodamas was the second dog and aimed for the small of the back. Oresitrophos bit into his shoulder. Then all the fangs, one after the other, struck the hunter's body as the man's body became the body of a magnificent stag. First, his favourite dogs: Ichnobates born in Gnosis, Malampus born in Sparta, Pamphagos, Dorceus, Oribasos. Then the enormous Nebrophonos, the quick Pterelas, the ferocious Theron, Agrius with his incredible sense of smell. Then Laelaps, Hylaeus, Poemenis, Dromas, Canace, Sticte, Tigris, Alce, Thoos. Then Nape, which is still a wolf, Ladon of Sicynon which is so skinny, Aello the indefatigable, Leucon white as snow, Harpyia and her two puppies. Then Lycisca and her brother Chyprius, Asbolus all black, Harpalos with a white spot on his forehead, Melaneus, Lacaena, Lacon, Labros, Agriodus. The very last one was Hylactor, whose voice was so unpleasant, so shrill, so piercing and it was the bone of Acteon's right hand, not yet transformed into a hoof, that he held between his fangs.

CHAPTER 71

The Cremation of the Past

War is less concealed than peace. States squander in war all their goods and sacrifice men without masking themselves any more. War defines unbridled humanity.

✣

On television screens, one could see the Muslim victims of Kosovo staggering along in single file to their rape, their separation, their death, submitting themselves to the sadistic euphoria of the torturers and the interests of the Western allies that asserted, to the rest of the world, that they were in the process of defending them. I was in Sens. My mother was staying with me for a few days and watched those lines on television. In the dumbfounded features of her face, I discovered that a sentiment stronger than fear, more pressing than the threat of death, had gripped her.

She was again moving forth in the exodus.

Dumbfoundedness does everything to bring the person who is dumbfounded nearer in space to that which dumbfounds.

She was trembling.

Something in the eyes goes to that which kills, even as the immobilized prey suddenly hears itself perishing in the more ancient jaws that it had seemed to recognize.

*

It's the aporia that lies at the heart of the thought of truth in Plato, *Meno* 80d: 'How will you inquire into a thing when you are *wholly* (parapan) *ignorant* of what it is; even if you bump into it, how will you know it is the thing you didn't know?'

This aporia is as beautiful as the triple question of Gorgias' *Treatise on Nothingness*.

One knows Plato's response, which is perhaps even stranger than the question he raises: One recognizes a thing of which one is *wholly ignorant* by means of the *memory* that it has left in the soul before the soul had the time to be constituted.

Inquiry is the sudden reminiscence (anamnesis) of a world anterior to atmospheric life, or to language, or to civilization.

An unexpected memory of the Erstwhile.

*

In the notes that Leonardo took while he was painting *The Battle of Anghiari*, war is defined as una pazzia bestialissima (*a most bestial insanity*). For Leonardo da Vinci, horses, dogs, birds of prey and men participated in the same way in combat. A sexual excitation appropriate to the whole hunting group, irrespective of species, presides over the spoils.

Even when modern, even when industrial, even when invisible, war participates in the hunt for the spoils.

As a spider web is woven, every State is a network of chains that control each other. Every chain, all the other chains. An immense and noisy mesh that enchains its links, and trembles. Both repressed impulse and enchained power: war and just as soon slavery. That which represses the unchaining enchains desire.

For the first time, in spring 1871, the machine gun was used to execute thousands of people in series. (During the Bloody Week, the machine gun enabled the Versaillais soldiers to get the better of 8,000–30,000 communards.) For Durkheim, this animal excitation was a 'collective effervescence' that was characteristic of human groups. However, it is not just a characteristic of humans. There is the most virulent possible originary power of 'everyone against one' that is accessible to any animal group.

The Romans spoke of a bacchatio characteristic of humans. This, too, is not characteristic of only humans. In this bacchatio remains a *leftover* of the frightening, flesh-eating, murderous unchaining.

Ut tigris. It's Medea. It's Dido. It's Agave. It's the Virgin Mary.

A mother holding in her arms a dead child.

*

On 11 August 1789, the Constituent Assembly abolished the royal and aristocratic privilege of hunting. Four days after the abolition, on 15 August 1789, the opening of the hunting season is voted for 'all people' in the 'manner of Saint Barthélemy of wild game'. This is how the frightening allusion to the Saint Barthélemy massacre was inscribed in the revolutionary law constituting the modern State.

CHAPTER 72

Stasis

The excitement of hunting for animal prey and the excitement felt during the lynching of a man whose guiltiness is dreamt (during the sacrifice of the scapegoat) not only combine but are enhanced in war. Because every nation defines a discrimination of foreigners, because every religion institutes a discrimination of unbelievers, all these violent voluptuous pleasures consecrate promontories, cliffs, bridges, lakes, streams, deserts, and thus are sublimated in monuments.

This sublimation concerns only the quarry and the spoils. (Everything used for killing, for expulsing, has become memorable through the blood that has been offered.)

It is the human crisis in person.

Fascisms, religions and nationalisms never hesitate about this matter: behind the bloody sacrifice in a group, there is the quarry of the hunt, and behind the quarry, the spectacle of the predation of big animals on the weaker beasts, be they human or not, which themselves, suddenly powerless, are fascinated when they fall in front of the eyes of the fascinators.

Ancient societies, like animal societies, are not exotic or foreign to those who stem from them. All of them, like those who stem from them, resemble each other. All of them are peopled with strange traces.

A silver coupe was found in the Regolini-Galassi tomb, in Cerveteri. It is dated ~650. An extremely dense imaginary meditation is concentrated on it. On the outer frieze, soldiers are marching. On the middle frieze, hunters are pursing animals. Inside the inner circle, two lions are fighting a bull. The thinking inscribed in this ancient image from the Neolithic period is categorical: inter-human war is peripheral, man-animal hunting lies in middle, and the non-mimetic heart is inter-animal predation.

*

This is the surprising description that Plutarch wrote about Caesar in *Pompeius* LI, 2: He considered the army to be his *own body* (autos sôma), and wars, in turn, to be like hunts (thèrais) and battues with dogs (kunègesiois).

This is political hysteria.

Political experience is the division, to the death, that marches on the group (that projects itself into time to maintain power).

It is what the Greeks called the stasis (civil war) that presupposes the krisis (the division).

He who loves power divides to reign, that is, makes the Reign come to pass.

It is what the Romans called civile bellum, civil war. Bellum comes from duellum. It is indeed the savage fraternal face-to-face which swirls around itself, endlessly turning, cleaving everything, swirling dizzyingly, ecstatically.

Romulus makes the furrow and with his two hands pushes Remus into the ditch born beneath the wall of Rome, which rises.

Warum Krieg? Unde bella? Bella delectat cruor. War adores blood. The violent destruction of other men plunged the men who carried this out into an excitement that was not comparable to that experienced during anterior predations. The delight in blood reinforces the blood-covered group, provokes an immediate contagion, induces an even bloodier response. This is the sexual impulse of death. This is why, in human societies, cruelty no longer has a beyond.

*

If women keep giving birth to the group in the blood that they retain or involuntarily shed (menstruation, childbirth), then men will come from voluntarily shed blood (sacrifice, war) building the male lineage.

The social paternity of men over the group is the sacrifice of single men in war. This passage must be at least *as bloody* as childbirth, which shows to everyone the maternity of mothers who, *by themselves*, reproduce *all* the group.

Men desired and still desire to steal from women the social reproduction that only they possess. This is what Bettelheim thought. He bore the magical, original name of Bethlehem, the place of Jesus' Nativity.

When he returned from the Buchenwald concentration camp, just after arriving in New York Harbour, he took a taxi, rang his wife's doorbell. She opened the door. She is embarrassed. She blushes. She hastily explains to him that she has started a new life. She closes the door. He is on the doormat in front of a closed door.

When he decided to die, he took a plastic grocery sack, stuck his head into it, knelt on the doormat, huddled up against the wooden door and tightened the sack.

CHAPTER 73

It is not in our power to put an end to the wars that are social feasts par excellence. We can only join the anti-tyrannical front of the dead who cry out in us.

Those who have been sacrificed, rather than martyrs.

Victims rather than heroes.

The city-less, the forsaken, rather than packs and armies in a row (that is, in order of battle).

*

During the heights of the Fronde, in 1652, the Solitaires formed a company to protect themselves from gangs seeking to pillage and shoot off their guns.

La Petitière, Arnauld, Pontis, La Rivière, Beaumont, Berri, with a sword at their sides and a musket on their shoulders, established guard posts in the oats and the nettles, where they took turns standing watch.

They had the impression of defending silence, solitude, the entrenched women, prayer, inaccessibility, the ancient ideals of the Roman Republic.

*

Otium and libertas, such were their values.

And such is my dream: a company of solitary individuals.

The only thing, to which I devote my hours and which is certain, is that reading, in the world, makes this dream come true every time that a book barely opens.

CHAPTER 74

René Descartes, Lord of Perron, a knight hailing from Touraine, son of Jeanne Brochard, especially dreaded armed Catholic bands. He hid in Germany at the beginning of the Thirty Years' War. He reached Holland, where he huddled up. He shut himself up in Hungary. He at last took a boat for Sweden, where he died in the snow. He wrote little books about the beauty of gales, hail, storms, the Alps. He would work very early in the morning, inside his book, in the darkness, then the half-darkness, then the half-daylight. He had his dream as Socrates had his demon. As Brutus had his spectre.

CHAPTER 75

Tacitus studied only one thing: the war of a few isolated individuals against the social subjection by which the empire was growing, the merciless battle, lost in advance, of a torch of light against the lies of every epoch. The book that haunted Tacitus might have had this title: On Solitary Individuals with respect to Packs, Wallows and Storms.

For Tacitus, time is loose, slack; history is dirty, melancholy; it rambles on about its manias; not only does it repeat, it also worsens what it repeats. Thus, endurance is not a virtue. On the contrary, what time undergoes—the patientia—is a kind of spinelessness. This is how Tacitus' life, under tyranny, was spineless and how his soul broke over this. It is with his own broken soul that he revisited the epochs which had engendered his own epochs and from which he stemmed directly. He thought: 'For want of knowing how to cut oneself off from words, from power, from contemporaneousness, from servility, one must convey a little of the force that reigned in the world before and make it surge forth again under the repetition of death. With a style that supplies the missing moral. A little of the Erstwhile must be reflected on the lake of Time.'

CHAPTER 76

Melanie Klein sought to ponder the abysmal destructiveness that takes place on the level of evolution and phylogenesis; she sought to ponder the dizzying originary void on the level of personal life and ontogenesis; she sought to ponder the kenosis on the ontological level.

The *lex talionis*, the law of an eye for an eye, shows an original feature in the development of the nursling because the nursling is a small prey that still eats its mother.

The first reality, for the baby who discovers the atmospheric world, is an unreal reality (in contrast to the reality of the first world that it has experienced), overwhelming (through its volume, its light, its noise, if the baby compares it to the dimensions of the modest water skin in which it has lived within a watertight first realm), unpredictable (through the brutal intrusion of atmospheric air into the whole volume of the baby's body), ferocious (through hunger, up to then inexistent or at least continually satisfied), incomprehensible (the inner mother having become external, the old site lost, terrestrial and celestial space suddenly replacing the dark, homogenous liquid world).

*

Companion in fortune
    If by chance you are asked:
    What is your regiment?
    'I am from the regiment of Swallow,
    Swallow, Swallow, Swallow, Swallow.'

*

The archaic ego craves the breast excessively. At the same time, the ego is afraid of being frustrated, terrified as it is by the evermore uncontrollable anxiety in which its hunger for the breast has thrust him. The ego is terrified to eat the breast that nourishes it. It is terrified to deprive itself, forever, of that which it loves and of she on whom it depends and who frightens it.

This is what to be *caught in a pincer movement* means. It is an aporetic pair of pincers. The two mandibles of the jaw are perpetually pre-symbolic.

It is the *double bind*, the contradictory double constraint, which throws one into turmoil by putting forth exactly contradictory arguments—an intersection that drives one crazy.

This double pressure is exactly *explosive* because it subjects one to two forces that are as violent as they are irreconcilable.

The intensity of its voracity—which the baby discovers only when it falls, like a little shipwrecked castaway, streaming with water and freezing, into the visible, atmospheric world—is anterior to the desire of satisfaction.

It is normal that the depths of the predatory universe are destructive because this world is racked as if by pincers by the devouring hunger.

*

Erstwhile, we ate without hunger. Then we swam. Then we ate *because of hunger* and our bodies were incessantly empty and became, little by little, because of this emptiness, personal (or at least personalizable).

Again, every six hours, time and the new emptiness, a fathomless emptiness, an emptiness that should thus be called natal, more than originary, open up in us—we who are cats, human beings, planarians, lobsters, taenias, flies, pikes, dragonflies, perches—and the hole in the middle of our white jaws emerges at the surface of the water and swallows the passing mosquito.

Desire is secondary with respect to hunger. Peace, fullness, satisfaction are only an intermediary episode. There is only one solution to the sadism of wild animals: depression, anorexia, isolation, culture. Melanie Klein: Beginning with the depressive position, the law of eye for an eye is finally replaced by guilt, in which we eat ourselves instead of the lactiferous breasts that attract our eyes on the torso of the women who made us and abandoned us.

*

The vulnerability of human beings seeking carrion in the slaughtering territories of the big wild animals has left in the soul an unappeased fear.

During birth, this unappeasable fear is added to the originary fright.

Erstwhile, a few millennia after the origin, the species was close to extinction.

In the ~25 million years period, Homo habilis wouldn't actively hunt for meat. He would eat whatever seemed comestible among that which he found at the intersection of his nostrils and the reddish fold of his lips. The volume of his brain was 500 cm^3.

In the ~350,000 period, the meat consumption of the Neanderthal man was 90 per cent. His diet had become comparable to that of a wolf. The volume of his brain was 1,600 cm^3.

CHAPTER 77

Circulus vitiosus deus

Çatal Hüyük, the first city, is a city built against lions, bison, snakes, mice.

A circle made of stones, dating to ~2,000,000 in the Olduvai Gorge. It is the most ancient refuge (a house for women and children) in History.

Predation derives from fascination, which itself derives from morphologic satellization. Bees and their extraordinary life are an endless dance around their nest. This dance is a nourishing language that comes back and calls out. The birth of language is hailed by predation. Language is a caller. Language is a predation even as dreaming in animals, before it invents itself, is a predation not of prey but of silhouettes of prey.

I presuppose a gravitation that is silent, flesh-eating, then linguistic, at the source of the back-and-forth round which invented dance, which invented the circle.

In his speculative rhetoric, Fronto says that human language (the languages) eats images even as bodies rip off flesh with their teeth.

*

There is a dance before dancing because a circle indicates, simply, the return to the sender. There is a mortal concentric sexual pleasure. There is an enigma of the founding torture of human groups gathering closely together, kneeling, raising their arms, murmuring, making themselves unanimous first around the torture victim, then gradually growing silent around the inert prey, just before the first word of the language that pronounces the emotion of the death in the eyes of the survivors who all encircle, silently, at least in a once-again imitated silence, the 'total silence' of he whom they have just put to death.

It is Isaac at the top of a mount.

It is Pentheus at the top of a mount.

It is Jesus at the top of a mount.

The words that are called human are those smothered cries that rise when the violence lapses. Each of them refers to a human being who is no longer.

*

The human species is spontaneously hallucinatory (much more than self-dissembling).

It is unconscious not in that it represses reality but in that it never perceives it.

Human beings rarely open their eyes on the terrifying anarchy of the human chronicle. Every catastrophe becomes, in human eyes, that is, in the depths of their inevitably linguistic memory, an ordeal that has a meaning. This meaning is that of satiety, that is, of peace. The social narrator (the myth) always defends the reproduction of the social order that he violently establishes in the site against the 'parasite' that he flushes out amid bloodshed and whose violent death and appearance he devours, all the way to its very memory. Every people distributes to itself its oriented facts, its associations after the event, its lies, its 'facta falsa', from language to language, that is, from community to community. The future is always good, the situation is positive, the group is mostly innocent, the children are mainly nice, peace will not be long in coming whereas it has never been present for a single hour.

*

The fact of saying is forgotten behind what is said.

The quod of language is forgotten in favour of the quid of thought.

The signifier is forgotten behind the signified.

The bloody sacrifice is forgotten behind God.

The social catch line is forgotten behind the father.

*

When the sexual fragments gather, the different, sexuated faces of the woman and the man mime self-inhibited chewing. They carrion each other tenderly. This is still called flirting—'flowering'—among those who feign to remain grass-eaters. But the word 'charnage' is an old French noun for a sexual union. In Latin, a sexual union was called unio carnalis. One incessantly needs to go back upstream into the Erstwhile of devourment.

'Acharnement' (relentless fierceness) strictly defines the acquisition of the flesh-eating spoils.

'Archarner' (to go at with relentless fierceness) means offering to the bloody flesh that emerges beneath the ripped-open hide.

'Acharner' a falcon, a dog—to get them to go fiercely, relentlessly at the prey—so that they will hunt.

We are a species that is 'acharnée', that has been made to go at fiercely, relentlessly.

In Christian populations during a millennium, the inter-dict of flesh (in the sense of red meat) corresponded to Friday, and the interdict of 'charnage' (in the sense of coitus) corresponded to Sunday.

*

When what is natural is driven off, it gallops back. ('What is bred in the bone will come out in the flesh.')

Throw out animality, and the human soul opens its anglerfish eyes and its tiger jaws.

Cover with clothes, fabric, silk, luxury, tattoos, jewels, bodies, and the ancestral ape-like nakedness suddenly surges forth from a slashed sleeve or a crease.

CHAPTER 78

The Empty Place

What was ferocity in animals became cruelty in human beings. What was perishment and devourment in animals became death and funerals in human beings. Cruelty is the sublimation of ferocity even as war is the sublimation of hunting, which itself was the sublimation of predation. Hunting and sacrifice are the two faces of the same infernal coin. This is the piece of bronze that is slipped between the teeth of the dead so it can be offered to the Ferryman. Its two faces form the unique symbol whose name is war. A symbol that is totally bloody on both faces. Two deaths have their double as humanity invents itself.

Carrion of flesh-eaters, mummy of the fellow creature, colossus of the sacrificed victim, statue of the god at the heart of the temple.

The sacrifice carves death into two big parts: fit for eating and unfit for eating, human and divine, edible (secular) and sacred (damned).

Damned, shameful, saintly, dangerous, untouchable, set aside for the ancient parasites of the 'erstwhile dividing up': eagles, wolves, vultures, hyenas, crows, etc.

*

There is never a present that is present: everywhere roams a dead interval. An empty place that is hunger then that is 'like hunger' and that roams from being to being. A lapse that is like Advent. A kind of waiting ever lingers between the lost and the imminent. The empty place that hunger hollows out in the depths of the body becomes the wall on which the dream is projected. Then this cave, which is an old jaw, gives asylum to the world of language. Therefore, it is always an absent living image that haunts behind the perception.

A vision which is a past, this is what the dream always is.

A past without presence which is like Being before Being.

*

'Entia prae entia' which form a 'Ja a dies'.

The Erstwhile ('Jadis') in relation to the past does not present the characteristic of having taken place. This is why Time does not belong to Being. The Erstwhile does not appear among the 'having been's' because it has not yet stopped surging forth. The Erstwhile is a more unpredictable geyser than everything that was. Everything that was has not made it happen or exist. It contains the *potentia* of all the possibilities. Just after the Second World War, Emmanuel Levinas put forward the hypothesis of an 'immemorial past'. He qualified it in three ways: (1) not representable, (2) what was never present, (3) older than the awareness-of. This immemorial past can be placed side by side with the fabulous embrace, which cannot be represented by he who results from it, which precedes conception, which does not have the position of a subject.

What Levinas called 'immemorial past' was perhaps ill-named: (1) because a past is not in question, (2) because memory is not concerned by it in any way.

The past is distinct from the Erstwhile in that the Erstwhile is the originary source, an ever-flowing torrent, a pre-real *fons* swallowed up into the nocturnal, explosive depths of the possibilitas in the same way as all the other stars that explode there and that siderate the rhythms of the earth, the melting of ice, the birth of beasts, the erections of plants, the explosions of volcanoes, the movements of the seas.

*

The 'true erstwhile' is that which is unknown at its source. In this source lies the explosion characteristic of past space and visible inside time.

It is inventiveness in its raw state—brutal, free, physical.

The 'fois' without 'autrefois'—the 'time' without 'in other times'—such is the erstwhile.

But is the 'true new' the Unknown?

Can the 'true future' be defined simply as 'one' of the 'other times' of time?

That which has had in its power not only the past but also all the un-carried-out possibilities of the naguère ('the formerly'), such is the Erstwhile that rolls its wave at the *edge* of the time that it enables.

The beginning begins upstream from space. At what instant does the beginning cease?

Perhaps in History.

Perhaps History should be called: There where the beginning ceases.

There where the past extends from the point where the beginning has ceased, History, in the mouth of human beings, can be called the hatred of Time.

Scolium 1. If time incessantly 'begins to begin' on the explosive background of the darkest sky, the distress characteristic of humanity depends on the compulsion of repetition (History) being stronger, in human societies, than the absolute newness of time. Societies prefer reiteration that is passed on, that is genealogical, linguistic and social, to unpredictable temporality. Groups favour the repetition of coituses and deaths in the perpetuation of faces, names, properties, goods.

Scolium 2. The secret of political passion is putting one's hand on reproduction, not on time.

CHAPTER 79

Polis

The time is long past when Jean Gerson wrote that the word 'police' defined the 'group of mortals in the order of time'. It was in the same period (in the 1400s) when Christine de Pisan wrote: 'The police assembles princes, noblemen, clerks, bourgeois, merchants, tradesmen, shepherds, and labourers.'

Back then, states were ranks.

Three radical states are superposed in any society. They can be defined in Spinoza's manner: unique, rare, numerous.

*

How is a city, a polis, an urbs, created? By killing one's brother at the very moment he leaps over the ditch.

How is a city peopled? By ravishing the women who live on the other side of the ditch, seeding them by means of systematic raping.

This, at least, is how Europe tells itself of its origin ever since its origin.

*

The Nile fish traps, which date back to the Palaeolithic period, immediately preceded the invention of labyrinths.

Enclosures from which the fish cannot swim back out.

Then nets in which the aurochs goes around in circles.

Human cities, palaces of Minos, parks for ferocious animals.

What were the first cities? Tombs. Their first inhabitants? The dead.

CHAPTER 80

Politeia

The threat that stands behind the sacrifice is: When will my turn come?

The political question par excellence is: What is the past that now puts forward its jaws?

*

Buddhism considers social functioning to be inherently bad.

The Taoists of Ancient China were the first who systematically meditated on anti-society.

In the last centuries of the Roman Empire, the fervour of the oriental monks of the Nile Valley, Palestine, Chalcedon, Syria and Mesopotamia gave birth to the increased use of a lifestyle which was completely new, solitary, city-less, contemplative, unsociable, and which they had copied from Indian ascetics. These monks were called either anchorites (that is, deviants), or 'apolis' (that is, the 'city-less' in the manner of blind, wandering Oedipus), or hermits (that is, living in the desert), or recluses (like animals that hibernate by huddling up under the ground or by curling up in the back of caves), or solitary individuals (like animals that leave packs and become solitary in nature before dying). After a noviciate of several years, the prior of the convent authorized the monk (monos in Greek, which means alone) who requested the permission, and who seemed to the prior to have the force to do so, to go away forever from the other members of the community. As Abelard wrote in his Latin: Monos unde monachus id est solitarius dicitur unam. (Alone, monk, solitary, makes one, means to be one). Either the solitary monk was locked up in a narrow cell with the door sealed, with only a miniscule window remaining open so that the most minimal amount of food could be passed through to him. Or he moved away from the tiny streets in which tradesmen lived and from the fields cultivated by labourers, and adopted for his home in the desert a cliff wall, a cave, an ancient cistern that had been closed up or was dry, an empty sepulchre, an unused slab of stone, a bulrush hut in ruins. The recluse devoted himself silently to his silence. The act of solitude sufficed to beseech a direct union with God beyond all social and even verbal mediation. The act of separation from the world of living human beings was in itself a human sacrifice without a knife, without an axe, without the spectacle, without blood, without war.

*

Stupefying centrifugal tradition from the dawn of, and outside of, human societies as they are in the process of constituting themselves. Shamans of Siberia and Ancient Japan, Taoist wanderers, Gymnosophists of India, hermits of

Memphis, ascetics of Heliopolis, Therapeutae of Alexandria, Roman anchorites, Christian monks, and at last men or women of letters in all places where languages had their double in writing.

CHAPTER 81

Natio

A Roman of the Republic would have been surprised by the ignominious meaning that could be attached, two millennia earlier, to the word natio. Natio like natura referred back to the fact of being born. The French word naître (to be born) exactly refers to the departure, by a little viviparous animal, from the female sexual organ following upon the sexual covering that has conceived it at the back of the uterus several months before.

Natus expressed the age of its advent in the group.

Nativitas evoked appearing into the light of the originary distress. This is how in Rome, in everyday language, the word nati meant children as opposed to parents. In its affectionate use, natus has the sense of carus, of dulcis, those ever-insane, belittling epithets that we use for calling those whom we love because they proceed from us, between our legs, like little pieces of fruit.

The 'nations' had this uniquely temporal meaning. They referred to broods. Among the peasants of Latiuim, the word natio exactly meant the 'litter of little ones born at the same time'. The naturalia were the name for the sexual organs of the two sexes at the source of the generation of children (at the source of the nascentia of the nati) coming into the world (natura) by broods (nationes). The metamorphoses, not of these words but of their meanings, were slow. It was at the end of the eighteenth century, in Europe, that colonialism and its particular ideology (romanticism, progress, science, hygiene, eugenics) reconstructed that which was originary, primitive, natal, archaeological. Little by little, they instrumented biology as ecology, genealogy as race, and all of this opened out into the extraordinary human horror that was the heart of the twentieth century.

*

The isolated life, like the singular experience, precedes birth. This root solitude lasts nine months for human beings.

Being integrated into humanity, like the acquisition of language, succeeds birth. This acquisition lasts several years for the little ones among human beings.

This is how the surging forth of humanity in the body is subjected to two kinds of kindling.

They are like two distinct hearths.

(1) the animal homo is the object of the birth (natus est) through which it reproduces its species based on the sexuation of those who precede it. The sexuation into two sexes signs the specific loss of every individual in death.

(2) the little one of the group succeeds his birth; it is kindled only in the 'mother' or 'national' language that it unconsciously acquires after the first eighteen atmospheric months. It begins to speak of itself in the third person. Little

by little, it consciously learns the language, it becomes ego-phoric (one who carries the ego into the dialogue) with the turnstile between the I and the you of the language that the mother teaches to her little one. This passing of the baton (this transfer of ego where the master is the you) occurs towards the age of seven.

On the one hand, the erstwhile in sexuality, on the other the past in language.

A double kindling (I am personally the witness of this). One must leave the in-fantia (the a-parlance) twice. One must light the 'parlage', the chattering, twice. To be born in a language and to take on a mother language, in order to acquire it, are two distinct experiences. The natus can stiffen into silence. He can regress, if one can distinguish at this pre-stage between regressing and turning around oneself, from right to left, from front to back, and sink into the soil like the little inhabitants of the seashore which leave, at the edge of the ocean, a little twist of sand at the surface of the perpetually wet 'path of God' where the sea comes and goes.

Where the sea 'beats'.

This little twist tempts the foot stepping forward.

The group *very willingly* stamps on it, ever since early childhood, when it consents *very willingly* to its dis-appearance.

*

(For one can prefer joining the marvellous, haunting din of the waves by progressing prudently *under* the sand that protects one from the visible world and *under* the seawater that comes back in timely fashion.)

*

The natio is the time when a same age group surges forth into the light of nature, breaking through the princeps solitude, breaking through a pocket of water in the light, attaining the atmospheric air that rushes into the solitary body until the vagitus, the first pulmonating cry.

Where does the problem of autochtony lie in the meditation of the nation? Nowhere. At an ancient date: nowhere. For what reason is all that is territorial, toponymic, land, fatherland, 'roots' so very little ancient? Because for millennia the human species knew no settled way of life. The predatory species follow the game that moves. Hunting societies do not settle: they follow their prey that follow their own prey that follow their vegetation and that follow the land that the glaciers uncover when they withdraw.

*

I remember that, one day, Levinas, although he was little inclined to making personal remarks during the classes that he taught us ('us' means his students, at the University of Nanterre, before the day of 22 March 1968), took it out on Ulysses, on the Greeks, on Joyce, with sudden violence.

'They all want to go home!' he said. 'What can a home of one's own be as a good? How can ontology pretend to be upstream from itself, as it were a lair? Even Plato wants a home of his own!'

Perhaps I am not exactly quoting Levinas' words, but the violence of his intonation was extreme. It still inflames me. It still moves me. I am not only writing down a memory. I thought that my mentor was going to stand up, leave the amphitheatre and abandon us in the very depths of Europe.

CHAPTER 82

Frau Kleinman

The Declaration of the Rights of Man specifies, in its third article: 'The principle of all sovereignty resides in the Nation.' The Declaration of the Rights of Man decrees, as a principle of human law, inter-national war between human beings.

*

Werner Scholem drove his sons out of his house. He said to them:

'You aren't patriots. You should be ashamed of wanting to leave Germany when it has gone to war. Our Jewish ancestors died in great numbers during the First World War when our country was threatened by France.'

After having cursed his sons in this way, Werner Scholem died in Buchenwald.

*

Freud wrote a totally insane, infernal sentence in 1930: 'Even if we don't feel at ease in our current civilization, all the same it is impossible for us to put ourselves in the shoes of an ancient galley slave or a Jew exposed to a pogrom.'

*

Frau Kleinman says to her son August at the beginning of the year 1933:

'Don't follow anyone's advice. Go away! Go away! Go away!'

CHAPTER 83

The emperor Marcus Aurelius liked spinning tops because they kept coming back.

Incessantly coming back.

Endlessly coming back.

Fronto mentions that one day he found himself at the emperor's side, during a visit to a grammar school. The emperor asked a young pupil, who was having difficulty learning his letters, for his spinning top. The child gave it to him regretfully. Fronto adds that the emperor of Rome never gave the spinning top, which he had confiscated, back to the very little child who was learning how to form letters by inscribing them from left to right on the wax tablet.

CHAPTER 84

Patriotism as a Little Toy

In 1889, Remy de Gourmont lost his position of librarian at the National Library after he had published an article, in the *Mercure de France*, with the title 'Le Joujou Patriotisme' ('Patriotism as a Little Toy').

CHAPTER 85

De desiderio patriae

In the 'nation', a settled way of life is not a defining criterion for the human species.

Extraordinarily, Christians claim to sojourn 'as if they were abroad' on the earth.

The Greek word that indicates a sojourn abroad is paroikia. The para-oikia is not the houses (oikia), but the house that is 'next to' the house: the stable, the hayloft, the pigsty, the sheepfold. The Greek word paroikia has given the Latin parochia, which has given the French paroisse ('parish'). The word does not seem to remember that it indicates that the district that it situates is precarious and that its essence is temporary.

'Parish' meant: For the Christian, there is neither nation nor fatherland. The only city acknowledged by the Christian is celestial. The place where the Christian aspires to live lies above the mountains and even above the vultures that fly over them and even above the sidera that determine them. On the earth, everything is immigrant suffering. The Fathers of the desert who, at first monks, made themselves into hermits, meditated deeply on the notion of parish. They defined the paroikia (the next house) as a diagôgè proskairos (temporary sojourn). This meant conceiving of it as a halt for a few hours. A stopover point for a day. They opposed the paroikia of the just to the katoikia of the nasty. They opposed the inn of pure opportunity, crepuscular, to the tyrannical forced colonization that the pagans exerted on the lands that did not belong to them (for only the Creator is the Owner). Even as pagans claimed often, and always wrongly, to be the autochthons of the lands they inhabited, Christians presented themselves everywhere as nomads whose fire and place by no means lay here below. The monks would say: Christians are like Abraham. When Sarah died at his side, she and Abraham were in Egypt. So Abraham asked for a bit of a grave for Sarah. He said to the sons of Heth:

'Peregrinus sum apud vos. (Here in your place, I am but a passing resident.) Let me have a piece of ground to conceal my love. I am not taking root with it. I am hiding my distress. I simply ask you for the authorization to conceal my wife from the vultures.'

I return to the death point that is in the face of human beings. The *vultus* is the space offered to the *vultur*. The painter Giacometti became obsessed with this secret point, in the centre of the human face, which the bird of prey is going to hollow out with its beak.

Many painters became devoted to this point, so *poignant* in the face of humans.

One saw this *ravage of progress* on the face of humans in the afternoon that followed the destruction of Hiroshima.

They were wandering in the August heat. They did not understand the nature of the evils that were striking them. They did not know they had survived the bomb called Little Boy, which had been dropped on the civilian population of Hiroshima to announce the good news that humanism had been restored on the earth. On the edge of the quay, black shadows were sitting in a row, without touching each other, almost naked, all of them with bloated bodies. On the main square, squatting on the sidewalk, there was a mother holding on her knees a very small child whose skin was dangling from its back. Both of them were motionless. They were so deeply stiffened into silence that no one could tell if they were still alive. In front of them, thousands of swallows with burnt wings were hopping, trying to drag themselves along the ground.

CHAPTER 87

Three of John Houghton's definitions.

In 1694, John Houghton called 'sport' a bear, a bull, a monkey, a horse once it was 'boited' (harassed) until it died.

In 1694, John Houghton called 'cokpit' the arena in which two cocks were made to fight after their wings had been clipped, their comb shaved, their spurs armed with iron.

In 1694, John Houghton called 'knock-out' the culmination of the 'sport': the combat was declared to be 'finished' once one naked man had fallen to the ground and could not stand back up.

CHAPTER 88

The Terror

At the beginning, Saint-Just did not use the word 'terreur' (terror), but rather 'épouvante' (great fear, dread). Saint-Just suggested: The idea of fraternity must be abandoned so that great fear is put on the agenda over the entire surface of the national territory.

It is Barère who had the poster printed, and he gave it the title: Terror is on the agenda.

Just as soon afterwards, on 5 September 1793, the Conventionnels (during the afternoon), judging in turn that the 'nation' was in danger, followed the proposition that Barère had made in the name of the Committee of Public Safety, making a pronouncement on the invisible insurrectional threat and solemnly declaring:

'Let us place terror on the agenda and thereby the royalists, the moderates and all the counterrevolutionary masses will disappear, in a single blow, at the same moment.'

In 1794, Robespierre puts forward the decisive argument:

'Virtue without terror is impotent.'

On 10 June, the Convention voted the law of the Great Terror after speeches by Couthon, then by Robespierre, then by Barère.

According to the law of the Great Terror, the defence of defendants is suppressed. Article 6 extends the category of enemy of the people to 'whoever will have sought to deprave morals'. Anything that does not turn its back to the Old Regime must be destroyed. Every bastille must be ruined. Châteaux must be dismantled. The churches of the Christians must be pulled down. The statues and all the treasures seized and melted down. All memory effaced in space. Even time must be new. A new calendar is needed because time begins. Anything that is not revolutionary is the enemy.

The oneiric—animal—functioning of the mind through an inversion of sequences (what goes from the predator to the prey goes from the prey to the predator) brings about the inversion of everything. The revolution of the former is the instauration of a world as the reverse side of the former one; it is the new world as the reverse side of the world.

Democratic Kampuchea prohibits money, dynamites banks, all the inhabitants of cities are transported to the countryside. All men and women become equals, rustics, blue, identical, and work the soil. Families no longer exist, nor individual or private or amorous or secret relationships. If you do not kill, you are killed. If you do not denounce, you are denounced.

*

With the French Terror, the Revolution was exchanged for sacrifice. Political passion reveals itself to be the ceremony of the exhibitionist, spectacular, starkly naked power to kill. It takes this ceremony characteristic of the State one hundred and fifty years to reach all the nations of Europe, then Siberia, then Asia.

*

Why do the Gospels written during the second century of the Empire of the Romans avow the mechanism of the emissary victim at the source of all religions?

Why did the Europe of the Enlightenment, during the eighteenth century, have the audacity to acknowledge the homicidal nature of every faith confessed by every religious community and desire to proscribe this fearful confidence in the invented gods who were reigning on the surface on the globe?

Why, on 5 September 1793, did the Revolution of the French avow the secret of social functioning to the world?

*

When power is called absolute, the term 'absolute' does not mean 'despotic'. The word absolute means 'absolutus', freed from all ties. This Roman expression defines the unique status of the emperor as 'princeps legibis solutus'. The prince is the unique citizen who is not subjected to the laws of which only he can act as the guarantor because he stands above them. The sovereign is the unique 'non-subject' of the empire. He is the only non-citizen.

The absolutus is the wild animal at the top of the human social pyramid.

No succession procedure, involving the emperor, can be made into legislation because he is spared of all law.

This is why, in Rome, well before the end of his life, the emperor must be sacrificed violently, *hunted down like a wild animal*, if one wishes his omnipotence to be interrupted.

*

The Terror defines the absolute State. With respect to the Terror, any non-killed citizen is a potential criminal. With respect to medicine, any adult human being is a child. His medical record follows his DNA samples, his blood type, his illnesses, his vices, his deviancies, his excesses, his fines, his income-tax returns, his bank accounts, his different cards relating to dependencies and services, his judicial record. The submission of expenses to the least costs turns all freedoms into *kinky* deviancies (suspected, perverse, narcissistic wasting). Power conceals control behind expertise, manages the after-effects of illnesses by obtaining the public supervision of them, measures the expensive gaps, bad dietary habits, the books consulted in municipal libraries and on the Internet, preferences in taste, sexual attractions.

All freedoms have once again become sins as they were in the former times of the Christian priests, after they had re-donned the black toga to symbolize mourning for the Empire.

*

History is not linear, because social time, whose origin is animal, is cyclic. Hunting, gathering and agriculture form circles like the movements, of the constellations in the sky, which indicate them or date them or announce them. Historical time is therefore circular, festive, repetitive, seasonal, obsessional, religious, mimetic, solar.

Theorem. Society tends to be circular. Regression is its lair. Bloody horror reconstitutes it because it reconstitutes itself in bloody horror. Its functioning is not rational. Its creation is not human. The secret Darwinism (I am not saying that it is a plan of life or a design of nature, I am suggesting that the idea of a plan or a design around which coming and massing together corresponds to social aspirations), which is a part of this horror, must not only be deplored because the societies in which we live prepare it. Every hour of the twilight watches the sun of 16 April 1975 setting. It must be said soberly: This horror awaits us in every instant because it is our face.

CHAPTER 89

The Passport for the Other World

One day, the earth itself became a 'nation' in space.

And a passport was needed to enter the other world.

Father Antoine Yvan, in his *Trompette du Ciel qui esveille les Pécheurs* (*The Trumpet of Heaven that Awakens the Sinners*, Paris, 1661), wrote: At last you arrive at death, which is the border of the other world. There the angels and the demons, having arrested you, examine you. They search through everything you are carrying; your spirit; your heart; your conscience; your thoughts; your words; your deeds; your omissions. Finally, they ask you for the passport of the Church, which is the absolution of all the sins you have committed; without it, you are lost.

⁕

Having papers. This oddity would have been inexplicable in times preceding our own. Socrates showing his papers before the Council of the Areopagus. Buddha holding out his passport to the fishermen and solitary individuals who would surround him on the banks of the Ganges. Jesus showing his papers to Pilate.

'Art thou the king?'

'Thou sayest it.'

⁕

The moderns attributed a new, painful meaning to the word paper.

This was, next to the body, touching the body, the written proof, on a piece of paper, of the existence of the body. In 1539, the Ordinance of Villers-Cotterêt organizes the stranglehold of the State on the organization of ages: the recording in parishes, on parochial registers, of baptisms, marriages, deaths. In 1792, parochial registers become municipal. In the nineteenth century, registering a baptism was transformed into registering a birth, which itself metamorphosed into an administrative identity number. On a piece of paper, the face is photographed, the genealogical name is certified and stamped by a police officer of the prefecture of the place where the card is issued, the subject is identified with respect to his language, sex, size, eye colour, blood type, profession.

*

Writers par excellence were paper beings.

Walter Benjamin, Walter Hasenclever, Stefan Zweig committed suicide because of this sudden Western quest for *life papers* in front of which books printed on paper, in which they had put their lives, were burning.

Ernst Toller hanged himself.

Karl Einstein took a rock and threw himself into the Gave d'Oloron.

CHAPTER 90

Heimatlosigkeit and Shamanism

There is no world conceivable here.

Heim, Hic, Home are not on earth.

There is no terrestrial home of one's own for the human figure.

There is time only for solitude only.

The journey of life to death is the Passover in the distress of two worlds articulated by birth.

It is the unsayable quest whose 'being-on-the-alert-ness' ('qui-vive') is born in the animal world.

One used to say 'chauvir' for this way of holding one's head, which, more than anything else in the world, I love to see emerging in nature. Then this word was lost. The verb meant at once suddenly pricking up one's ears with one's head immobilized, one's neck stiff, one's face tensely stretched outwards, while waiting for breaths, odours, voices.

Then, slowly, to aim one's eyes towards the abnormal noise or the disturbing movement taking place in the distance.

Unheimlichkeit (disturbing strangeness), Heimlichkeit (the secret hiding place), Heimlosigkeit (homelessness, statelessness) share the Heim.

*

Linguistic clandestineness (nominalism), intimate clandestineness (secret sexuality), territorial clandestineness (political divergence) add up to a form of exile, more than to a form of the world, on an earth where everyone among us emerges in an isolated state.

*

Every night I loved the night like a peace made of silence and blackness. Like a refuge more ancient than myself. I don't know how I had obtained permission from my family, when I was a very little child, to eat in darkness. Something restive, a fright, a kind of being-on-the-alert-ness, were associated with the difficulties that I was experiencing to live. It was as if my resources, my anxiety, all my attention were *natively reared up* when coming up against anything that sought to impose familial power and to organize linguistic potency on all things and on every living being. I managed more or less to thwart the reprobation that I saw was attached to the activities and to the odd habits that had started to bewitch me and, at the same time, enabled me to isolate myself.

Later, having survived, after having gone over the border of social and political majority, I wanted to endeavour to meditate on the originary character of asociality. I sought to analyse and to collect all the divergences ever since the dawn of historical time.

As it turned out, this movement that had been presented to me as against nature, or as slightly psychiatric, or as possibly anomic, was the very origin.

From the outset, the first social specialization (shamanism) was exclusion, antinomy, anomy, periphery. Those that had remained on the side of the animals, of savagery, of solitude, of the origin, made the others associate against them.

＊

The shaman belonged to the margins of the world. He was the one who untangles the evil spell. He would unshackle whoever was enchanted.

A counter-world of forces stands behind all the forms that appear in this world. Forces (of blood, of sperm, of breath, of wind, of torrents, of tides, of dawn) irrigate the morphological appearances of all of nature. One must harness the force of the volcano that gushes up in the mountain, that of the ocean that swells in the tempest, that of the stag in rut that ejaculates its big sprays of semen into nights that are longer and darker at the end of autumn, that of trees, of bushes, of vine stocks that cover themselves with leaves and suddenly spread out in spring.

Any rarefaction of wild game, any sterility, any desert, impotence, famine, unhappiness, illness or death is a lack of force that one must remedy by going back to the first world of forces.

One must go and alone seek over there, beyond the visible world, beyond the known world, in the territory that has never been seen, in the adventurous forest, in the origin, under the skin, in the heart, in the stomach, in the cave, the force that is lacking here.

*

Çaman is an old Tungusic word that refers to the soul-carrier. Death is the animal mouth that opens its jaws from the ground all the way to the sky. Death ravishes. Illness ravishes. The soul has been stolen. It must be found again and put back in place. The shaman is the solitary specialist of counter-ravishing. He goes all alone among the dead and comes back all alone—for one always dreams alone—bringing back the lost soul.

*

Stylus, stylo, pen, penholder, small soul-holders, soul-carriers.

A witch astride a sprig, a penis, a finger, a tanbark twig, a broom. They are magic fairy wands, life-carriers, inaos, border-passes, soul-carriers. For it is only a 'woman' who can reorganize the world 'here' by travelling in the world 'over there', as was erstwhile the case.

Woman, because the origin is feminine—and still more maternal than it is feminine.

The woman at the origin is the Skin that clothes. A donkey skin that conceals, the solar skin of the world, the moon skin that metamorphoses and time that progresses.

Since she has been the skin that clothes, she is clothed in all the sewn-together hides of the hunted animals. She wears the antlers of a member of the deer family as a headdress. As in sleep the inhabitant of the dreaming brain, the female shaman leaves the visible earth for an invisible world. She leaves the domesticated for the wild. If the shaman is a man, then he is insane because this is the only proof that can be found, in the group of men, that a body has been aggressed by the wild force and that he has travelled outside this world. He has been wounded; he has mutilated himself; he has suffered; he devours everything that is prohibited; he has been initiated by the counter-world in which he has travelled; he always does the opposite of what everyone does—but he has survived.

*

The 'contraries' refers to the shamans among the Zunis (they are called Contraries or Inverses because they do every backwards).

Among the Sioux, only men struck by lightning can go to find the Thunder Bird.

They are called the 'Bizarre Ones' among the Kalash.

They were called the 'asocials' in the Atlas, in Morocco, at the border of those extraordinary painted cliff walls at the base of stone forests, at the shadowy and coolest limit of the sand.

All these denominations define a same margin as far as territory is concerned, a same periphery, in terms of home, a same exclusion from the group.

Every shaman, every fairy, every sortilegus, every witch was astride the borders of worlds (visible and hidden, human and animal, feminine and masculine, amniotic and atmospheric, alive and dead).

*

The Middle Ages were haunted by the cavalcades of women in the clouds, in the forests, over the heaths, on the edge of cliffs. To be truthful, the Roman canon law did not speak, at the end of the Empire, of 'spell casters', of 'witches', but of 'women who proclaim that they ride at night on certain animals, accompanied by Diana, Herodiana, Herodias (in Old Norse, Dainn, Heredainn), and who cross vast invisible spaces in no time at all'.

The trance of those women is called journey (seidhr).

I was filled with wonder the day I discovered that the counting rhyme *Am stram gram pic* ('Eeny, meeny, miny, moe') preserved, intact as it were, in its French sequence, the Siberian rhythm of the shamanic drum *Emstrang Gram*.

The antique incantation of the wolf (which is called gram in Old Norse), in its expanded form, is the following:

Emstrang Gram

Biga biga ic calle Gram

Bure bure ic raede tan

Emstrang Gram

Mos!

The 'tan' (tanbark) is the magic wand.

The 'tan' in Old Norse is called, in Old French, the fairy's 'brin' (sprig, twig, wisp).

If grain or gram, in Norse, is the name of the wolf, 'Mana gram' means the wolf of the Moon. In the sky, wolf refers to the evening star that chases after the moon to devour it. The wolf is the devouring beast of Hell: Hel, Hell, Helle, Hellequin. 'Grain' can still be read, in French, in Isengrin, which refers to the gluttonous wolf in the *Chanson de Renard*. The incantation can now be translated word by word:

Always-strong Wolf

Come come I call Wolf

Arrive arrive I ask the tanbark

Always-strong World

Eat!

CHAPTER 91

'Hurler avec les loups'—to follow the pack of wolves and howl with them. This expression is not only French. It is prehistoric. It is Palaeolithic. It is as ancient as the invention of hunting. It is as vast as Siberia and Lake Baikal. The only truly prohibited thing in social life: do not follow the pack and howl with the wolves.

Democracy: the greatest number of howling wolves dictate the howling of everyone.

The essence of morals: he who does not howl with the wolves is devoured by them.

*

Pre-social polarization brings face to face the compact group of those who increase the hold exerted on themselves and the much less numerous group (much more frayed, more messed up, more frightened, in frantic retreat) of those who seek to extricate themselves from the grip of the group by going back to the origin.

The hatred of cities begins very early in History. It begins with cities themselves, surely—but perhaps even this loathing against the focalization of homes around fires begins *before* the hamlets themselves, because it seems that one can read, on the Palaeolithic cave walls, an opposition between gregarious and solitary individuals.

Beginning with the first homes where fire is domesticated like a violent, skittish beast, beginning with the first well in the cave of Montignac, with the first well in the Torah, with the first well in the Henan Forest, a solitary human being dies. A nameless man, his arms thrown back over his head, falls backwards at the source of the human world. Jacob is forced to flee from his brothers, Zhuang Zhou moves away, Epicurus moves away, Pliny moves away, Saint Basil moves away.

Even the emperor Tiberius moves away.

The great mystics are the great unsaddled individuals, the great thrown-back individuals, the great imprisoned individuals, the great excommunicated individuals: Master Abelard, Master Eckhart, Hadewijch of Antwerp, The Blessed John of Ruusbroec, John of the Cross.

It is not that the hermit, the asocial individual, the non-speaker, the infans, the wild child, the autistic person, are human possibilities, the object of my curiosity: it's the zoological source that inexhaustibly flows into them.

It is the fact that what unsaddles in the emotion, as at the natal instant, brusquely tears open the natal link and *makes one leave one's place* within the space of the group.

CHAPTER 92

Paulinus and Therasia

When it was learnt in Rome that, at the age of forty, Paulinus—among the foremost personalities of the Empire, the head of one of the most considerable fortunes of the city, the owner of great landed estates, the master of whole provinces, a former consul—was giving up urban and mundane life, giving away everything and abandoning the century, the scandalized patricians unanimously rebuked him.

What was the Empire—threatened at its borders by the barbarians flocking from the east and from the north of the world—going to become if the inheritors of the greatest families themselves abandoned the world in which their ancestors had reigned? If the most valiant renounced weapons? If the richest failed to lend support, leading their own clientele in their wake and breaking up the provinces under their jurisdiction?

Time went by, but the hatred aimed at the young senator did not lessen.

Paulinus even sensed, as the days went by, a dangerous hostility growing against him.

The desire to kill made some throw stones at him as he walked through the streets, he who had renounced his litter and horses.

People would spit behind his back when he had gone by.

As the heading of his letters, these touching words can be read: 'Paulinus et Therasia peccatores . . .'

Paulinus and Therasia, sinners, we love you. The moment had come to say farewell to you, you who were so dear to us, etc.

*

The patrician, who had turned himself into a hermit, did not have to wait long for his revenge.

In 410, Paulinus heard in the distance a great din coming up from the valley.

Paulinus left his leafy cabin.

Overcome by curiosity, Therasia followed her husband.

Both of them saw frightened, miserable, famished columns of runaways arriving on the road leading to Nola. Then Alaric's hordes surging forth on horses, stamping over the harvests of the estates, pillaging the countryside villas, besieging the walled cities, setting fire one after another to their suburbs and all the territories of the provinces.

However, when everything was annihilated, nothing that Saint Paulinus saw saddened him.

*

In the senate, Paulinus, wearing again his purple-hemmed toga, had not declared to the senators: 'Conscript Fathers, I renounce the century.'

The fabulous expression 'saeculo renuntiare' dates back only to 533. It appears in an edict of the emperor Hadrian. From there, it was copied and put down in the Code of Justinian. This expression is extraordinary in that 'renouncing the century' means 'renouncing History', which does not indicate 'renouncing Time'.

In the same way, abandoning the worldliness of the world by no means signifies leaving the earth.

A human being 'dead to the world' does not mean 'no longer alive'.

He who resigns ceases to grant the service that he gave until then, but his willingness is not to extinguish his life: simply, he gives back his mission. In the renouncement, the giving up is, first, a kind of scorn before being an abandonment with respect to the group and a prodigious abeyance as far as the solicitation of the species to all constraints is concerned.

*

In the Middle Ages, 'to renounce the century' was expressed according to four modalities: leaving the social world and the role that one played there; no longer subject oneself to the judgement of living human beings and no longer recognize any intra-mundane authority; interrupt duration as a genealogical posterity by practicing celibacy or by imposing chastity upon oneself; tear up the secular, glorious, political, military, cultural narrative of History by abandoning the competition for positions, rewards, riches, titles, tombs, memorials.

*

For all human beings bend dangerously under the honours, like bamboos under the weight of snow.

CHAPTER 93

Praeteritio

Time is that strange governing authority in which nothingness calls out to the living. In Paul's First Epistle to the Corinthians 7:29, he wrote: That they that have wives be as though they had none. Et qui habent uxores, tanquam non habentes sint. For the figure of this world passeth away. Praeterit enim figura hujus mundi. These sentences might have been those of a Buddhist in India: The house is on fire! Go away! Go away! They could be those of a Taoist: May those who are truly pure not add a stain to nature. May they keep themselves from soiling what they contemplate. They could be those of a Tantrist: May they swallow even their semen! May those who live in this world make use of it as if they were unable to use life. For it is incessantly effaced in the depths of the sky, like the image that does not exist at the beginning of ourselves.

This is how religious experience wants the world to disappear.

This is how the apostle who invents resurrection strews the earth with the *past*.

Praeterit enim figura hujus mundi.

He spreads the world as 'past'.

'Ever past', the figure of this world.

Destruction commands them to their death.

The proper mode for the collective existence of human beings is the *preterit*.

*

Who remembers the dates for times of peace? Dates of peace cannot be remembered. Vengeance and memory love each other. Those covered with blood create markers like red lights at intersections. Every society is a cult of the dead. Genealogy aims only at the past. What could it envision other than the past? The *praeteritio* is not only what invisibly passes by in the passing of time, but the fact of not bringing anything onto the testament that is of the order of a genuine heritage.

*

The witness tests. This is why de-test means to tear the survivors away from their testimony.

The 'sacrorum detestatio' is the solemn renunciation of the familial cult of 'imagines' (the images mean the heads of the fathers), which takes place in front of witnesses.

If 'to attest' calls the gods to witness so that they listen to the prayer that is addressed to them, 'to detest' beseeches them not to take into account what has been said and advises them to look away.

Testa is the head. Testis is at once the testicle, the witness, the referent, the test. The etymology of the Latin 'test' is 'tristis': he who stands as a third party (the chorus, the assembly, or the god). The witness (testor) brought his testimony (testamen) in front of the assembly of the people, inside the temple, before the god. The survivor is called the superstes: he is the witness who has passed through the detestable horror (the kind of horror in front of which there are no longer but eyes looking away). The superstes (the remaining witness, the survivor, the pious one, the superstitious one) is he who brings the tabulae testamenti (the tablets of the testament) sealed by death.

*

It is odd—odd in that it is universal—that the erotic erstwhile of each human body is banned from the social world. In novels, no one eats and no one defecates. Coitus and hunger have *passed* into language. This is the preterit. A structural social agony is healed by means of a feast. A human feast is always a putting to death that pretends, each time, in language, to bequeath to the participants something else than the prey that they are devouring. Either something entire (war, racism, crusade) or an element (laughter, sacrifice, love). Always a prey or a bloody red rag tossed out to the hunger of a predator. How can order be re-established in the uncontrolled expansion of disorder? By means of something or someone killed, which re-establishes order because it makes one forget the violence in the cult of death. The cult of Caesar was born from the sacrifice of Caesar by means of seventeen knife stabs. The cult of Jesus was born from the sacrifice of Jesus by means of three big nails and the point of a lance. Every monarchy comes from a living dead person to whom is added the superscript numerals XIII, XIV, XV, XVI. If the rite defines the first imitation of the sacrifice, then the sacrifice must always be attributed a zero. This zero is the language, that is, the self-concealment of the functioning of human societies.

Satiety itself is a self-concealment of hunger.

Pleasure itself is a self-concealment of desire.

A religious mass and theatre pretend to purge the violence that they show and, by showing it, they restore it.

In what way can one say that the religious mass lies? The death of the blood-covered god is there. However, the church, the rite, the shadow make everything flow back into the hymns.

In what way can one say that tragedy lies? The blood-covered dead, sword in hand, are there, and what is worst in social functioning and its contradictions is exhibited. However, these are strangely forgotten amid the beauty of the sentences that name them.

＊

The self-concealment of social reproduction (sexuality) refers to the self-concealment of the sexuated reproduction in death (mortality sorts out the sexuated in time).

But self-concealment is not what should be said. It is the word obliviscence that should be brought back to life. The Romans possessed a verb to express this supple, voluntary, active effacement of consciousness in knowledge or in habits or in usages.

Obliviscor ('obliviate') means to no longer daydream.

Humanity stares neither at the sun, nor at a personal death, nor at parental coitus, nor at the founding murder.

It is not said 'Caesar run through by seventeen knife stabs, including a mortal one given in his groin by his son', but rather: 'pax romana'.

*

Beginning with its 'non-disorder', order cannot meditate on its brutal source (of which it is the *reaction*). Beginning with its 'peace', it cannot meditate on the totally contingent and disorderly violence of its birth.

One who is discriminated is without regard for the discrimen.

Even as the puer, in whom sexuality has been made latent, cannot ponder the erection of his father's genitalia and the dilatation of his mother's vagina as they are riding each other and then letting their semen and fluids flow so that by blending they will conceive him. This imagination is even what the adolescent boy or girl who reaches the genital world detests the most.

Thought vanishes in front of its source and mislays it.

Violence devours itself by devouring the victim who interrupts the civil unleashing of the violence. By turning around, retrospection already transfigures the scene that it reconstructs.

Sense stands in the way of the signifier that produces it.

Human societies remain in the automatic, minimal orbit, which is not, strictly speaking, conscious, of the animal societies from which they derive.

There is a cyclic, seasonal nature of the sacrificial human culture dominating them to which they yield, violently, without understanding it.

*

To society, preterition.

To individuals, the unconscious.

*

A struggle must be engaged—with no returns on the investment—against the social. But it by no means must be engaged as one against all. It must by no means be envisaged as a scapegoat who would guarantee unanimity by piling up stones in the held-out hands of those who aim at it. It is not a matter of engaging in an unequal struggle so as to perish in it. One must engage in a secret life to survive. These are La Boétie's words before he died, before his friend betrayed him, before Montaigne renounced to publish him, before oblivion attained him. It is Spinoza excommunicated, banned, a fugitive, free, polishing the glass of his magnifying lenses to see more closely the happiness that animates the earth below the human world and to contemplate as long as possible the original explosion that continues in the depths of the celestial vault. Some human beings escape from the myth, rip through the voluntary servitude, wander on the periphery of 'All men'.

CHAPTER 94

In the main hall of the Gare de Lyon, quai des Chiffres, to take the train to Sens. The poor, the beggars, the 'Apolis' (the city-less), the Foreigners, the Homeless, the seated Wanderers, the bums were struck with truncheons, were dragged along the ground by their armpits, were heaved up into vans by armed men with black truncheons and wearing electric-blue uniforms. Where are the tales where the accursed entered palaces and simply said to the guards: 'I am a foreigner'? Foreigner was back then the most beautiful word and it opened doors. Hospitality was a duty, not even a virtue. The foreigner would sit down at the best place next to the king, to his right, like a sun appearing in the world, eating and drinking his fill. Then he would turn to the king and ask:

'Sire, would you like to know why my chin is shaved and why I'm missing an eye?'

And the king bowed down in front of him and said:

'Tell me, tell me, my friend! What adventures have been yours?'

CHAPTER 95

Anachorèsis, Analysis, Ablösung, Seccessio Plebis

Paul wrote in 1 Corinthians 4:13: We are made as the filth of the world, and we are the offscouring of all things unto this day. The Greek word that Paul uses in his epistle is katharmata. It is translated into Latin by purgamenta.

Like pods and hides, pieces of wood, and heads.

Like the oblivion of the Hebrew, Babylonian, or Greek languages.

Like the impossibleness of Jerusalem.

Like the lostness of time.

The fragmenta, the purgamenta, are 'things without being'. They are beings that no longer have unity in being. They are like all the aphorismena, like all the segregata, like all the excluded from the other part, like all the sexuated when they do not submit to the other sex.

*

It is possible that the passiveness into which plunges individual shame, or the weakness to which social humiliation is devoted, or the vulnerability that is established, hour by hour, by solitary contemplation, explore more the condition of humanity than the pride of belonging, the power struggle within the group, the hateful, bellicose, crowd-forming functioning that comforts the group.

*

'Ragots' (pieces of malicious gossip) used to refer to wild boars. Ragere. They rage.

Legendary flashy rags, sexual anecdotes, scraps of light, 'ragots' are those strange fragmenta that snort like hogs once they begin to be in the sty.

Craving defines the unremitting effort to rage, to overturn what struggles to remain standing. To destroy beauty. To tear from hands that possess it the object that cannot possessed—nature itself is the object that not one of its members possesses—and to shatter it in front of everyone.

Craving is the mass of warriors lined up at Soissons. It is the demos. It is the entire group of those who drool in the grip of a hunger that they don't have the courage to satisfy on their own. It is the entire group of those who, at first black, begin to become pink. They argue over a vase and shatter it.

*

Aphorisms: the sexes.

Anchorites: the souls.

Asocial individuals: the desires.

*

When Freud asserts that every individual should devote himself to the great task of undoing himself from his parents, the word that he employs is Ablösung. Here is the order: analysis begins by desubjectifying the subject. The desubjectified person disaffiliates himself from the genealogical kinship. He becomes an individual within the social group. European analysis makes wolves.

*

In the evolution of religions, there is a splendid perverse point that makes them suddenly overturn. There is a moment, which seems vertical, which appears irresistible, and which makes them withdraw little by little from the social world that they have, however, contributed to organize and spread. Early on, Christianity, like Buddhism, founded the movement of political withdrawal, of religious specialization, of the delocalization of rites, of the denationalization of faith, of the universalization of the message. Very quickly they tore priests away from direct bloody sacrifice, made them dedicate themselves to the sexual non-reproduction of the groups that they taught, established monasteries in which they placed the most pious men as anchorites, banned their bodies from the other bodies through chastity, radicalized their destiny by means of pure study, which is the most beautiful state of prayer.

This is how religion little by little leaves behind the courts and the urban centres. It reaches the periphery of the civilized world and withdraws from its markets. It chases the merchants from the temple. It liberates itself from the authority of princes. It disengages itself from all warring or secular functions, frees itself from its grandiose ceremonies and immense pilgrimages that it convokes in a given space, abandons sacrifice, magic, fasting, interdicts, benedictions, miracles, exorcisms, changes, vestments. After having left its monuments, after having practised solitary asceticism, the mystic founders at last in a world of purely internalized faith whose infinity is no longer subjected to anything.

This world is no longer anything but a black hole, black and internal, black like a mountain cave, asocial, ante-linguistic, ecstatic, secret like its origin, like the poor source of the nativity.

He who falls into ecstasy, he who reads, he who loses, he who loves—true love is a direct intimate relationship, also asocial, also a black hole, without a heed for the century nor for the gaze of other human beings, nor even for the beloved.

It is Augustine's phrase: God more intimate to me than I am to myself.

Therefore the divine part corresponds to the asocial part.

*

The metamorphosis of the world of Jews in the first century was radical.

Where a temple no longer stood, a school was built where one could learn how to read.

Sacrifice was extinguished in reading like the gold of the sun in the twilight before it sinks into the night.

*

The alone, the singular, the singularis porcus, the 'singlier'— such is the curious 'erstwhile' that hides behind the French word 'sanglier' (wild boar).

The 'singlier', among the old solitary boars, is to be distinguished from the ragot, the goret (piglet), the marcassin (young boar), the truie (sow).

He who is solitary is more radically singular than the individual.

He who is singular is more alone in the forest than the individual in the group. It is not a subject in a dominated-dominator group, it is the *limes in confrontation* (the frontier in confrontation). Hirsute, obstinate, he who is solitary represents, in the eyes of human beings, the irreducible willingness to defend himself against anything that comes to face him. To stare hard at anything that surges forth. He hears everything living head-on. Like the representation of the night owl. Such is the Palaeolithic appearance of that which is Alone. It's Medusa. During the past millennia, the boar is the only prehistoric animal that has increased in numbers *despite the human species*. From the garrigue to the forests, from the mountain to the saltus more or less cleared by grubbing and then abandoned by peasants to the wild exuberance and to the forest, its mobility, its speed, its endurance, the excellence of its flesh, the tireless force of the beast that was called the bête noire, its motionless confrontation fascinated, alerted, instructed. Saint Anthony said: The anchorite goes onto the saltus where he usurps the areas of the wild animals that lived on the earth before God had made him out of clay with his hands. Usurp the lost area. Invent a false life for yourself. You must open a file-lure in order to offer to predators names where they will stop and addresses where messages will go lost. Nourish their hatred with a destiny that leads them astray. You, if this is possible, don't immediately reach the ash and spruce trees, don't climb up the mountain slope where you would expose yourself, remain in the eye of the cyclone where you will best be concealed. Flee without moving, wherever you are and you will live the most peaceful life. Go from alley to alley, then from back courtyard to back courtyard to find again the dust of the coloured Skira painting sticks behind the Saint-Martin Canal. Slip between the plants and the spindle-trees, hide behind the bamboos of the flower shop on the rue Buci, to go up the interminable spiral staircase, to finally arrive, under the roofs, in Cremonini's ramshackle studio. Progress among the ruined high-rises of the 93rd district, the smashed-open dustbins, the burnt-up cars, the out-of-order lift, the broken windowpanes, and push the door of Rustin's studio. I unsubscribed from the telephone company and, with the same gesture, from internet so as not to be reached by any kind of obligation. My e-mail address was resorbed in an instant on the computer screen like mist on window-pane when winter is interrupted. I severed the electric wires of the doorbells. I ate hazelnuts and all the fruits of the season while drinking wine from Gex or Bellegarde. Ever less fruit. Always more wine. I would doze off wherever I was reading. I would travel without moving, wherever I was. The great journey is not really sedentary or, rather, it takes place in a 'non-place', it takes place in a corner of any-where, it takes place in the angle of a wall, it takes place in the non-space, it takes place in time.

When one stops submitting oneself to the judgement of those from whom one has entrenched oneself, everything that wounds frays and is erased in a stroke, like haze over the river at the moment when the sun rises.

CHAPTER 96

One Must Reject the Gaze of Others

Miss Draper educated Colette's daughter in this way: 'You must not cry in front of a man or a woman, must not imagine going to the toilet and keeping the door open.' Michel Foucault wrote in *Society Must Be Defended: Lectures at the Collège de France*: 'There is no other first or final point of resistance to political power other than in the relationship one has to oneself.' There is a funereal zeal in the willingness to be happy in every moment in the eyes of those who are not any happier than you and who, like you, tremble about dying. Stop compelling yourself to appear as winners in a game where the outlay is in advance, before your very eyes, deducted from your days! Everything is a loser, everything is lost, everything is fragile, everything is rare and everything is becoming less plentiful, becoming rarer, becomes a splendour. A splendour that is all the more radiant in that it becomes rarer and more scattered. Shamanism, anchoritism, Catharism, Jansenism, anarchism, Buddhism, Epicureanism, hermitism, Gnosticism, Christian monachism—there were so many good things to take in this world in front of those sad faces. Everyone denounces what is negative. However, the negative is the pearl of mankind. It is the talisman of art. 'No' is the most beautiful word in the world. Ever since the end of the Second World War, ever since the dropping of bombs on the islands of Japan, ever since the end of the Vietnam War, ever since the end of the Khmer Republic, ever since the timid, hesitant and unaccomplished end of the Communist dictatorships, it has become a sin in the United States, in England, in France, in Rome, in Berlin, in Tokyo, in Shanghai, not to be positive, at the minimum and, if possible, one should beam all over one's face. Even as discourse has for its distinctive feature to oppose differences, and judgement for its distinctive feature to dismiss oppositions, while both neglect the gap lying between what is opposed and what is different, they dig ditches into which one is forced to fall, naked, leaving the shovel and the horror to he or she who weeps and follows. For millennia, societies have created many more outcasts, beggars, rebels, galley slaves, deserters, heterodox individuals, non-believers, outlaws, bandits, poor people, Conversos, Moriscos, Lutherans, smugglers, Comuneros, Agermandos, bachelors, sick people and insane people than are suitable for them. When Foucault desired to establish the archaeology of these extraordinary and impalpable 'silences' that are gradually generated by ideologies as they take over the myths that preceded them, he revealed the abysmal, artificial, systematic, bloody, dizzying gap that every new rampart, as it is built, opens at its foundations at the same time. The extreme experiences that are the distinctive features of historical Western civilization had been the orgy, insanity, dreaming, sex. The opposition between Apollo and Dionysus resulted in the prohibition of bacchanals in Rome. The opposition between reason and mental disorder resulted in the locking up of the insane in the asylums of the Renaissance. The division between sentimental love and sexual voluptuousness resulted in the prohibition of masturbation, brothels, paedophilia and all erratic, animal, fantastic or fantastical practices. Prisons, the police, the ordering of discourse, the will to know, the obligation to say, tribunals, asylums, hospitals, maternity hospitals, the press, television, military service and the State are violent like the violence of the dialogue itself in which everyone would like to be heard in the trap of the other. Even as human society turns speakers into silent people, language invents the humiliation of little children who do not speak with respect to the adults who instruct them in the discourse of the group, who subject them to the struggle of the dominant classes against the inferior classes and organize them into a hierarchy of the sedentary and the stray, of the domesticated and the wild, of the castrated and the savage, of culture and nature. Such are the two cities. Such are the two realms. Such is the division characteristic of viviparous animals. Between erstwhile and past. Between urge and memory.

CHAPTER 97

The Epoch

The French word époque comes from épochè. This is why it is impossible to be the contemporary of anything in this world. Even at the most intensely close moment of love, one does not know of what instant the time, which one is in the process of experiencing, is contemporary because one is the fruit of the scene that one is creating. In ancient Greek, the word épochè simply meant halt. To be at a halt like a dog at a halt (and awaiting the order to chase after the prey). To be at a halt like a stag at a halt (and ready to bound off in flight from any predator who moves into the field). To be at a halt is to perk up one's ears. In Antiquity, the sceptical philosophers called épochè a sudden suspension during their research. In our time, philosophers refer in French by means of épochè to the fact of putting in parentheses ego, object, world, and of examining what emerges, without having recourse to preliminary knowledge.

But the word épochè can be emphasized in a much deeper way. The epoch can be deeper. One must stay in Antiquity. It suffices to add, to Sextus Empiricus' lesson, the command of Jesus quoted in John 7:24: Nolite judicare. 'Do not judge' does not only mean 'Abandon the search for truth', but also 'Abandon the internalization of society in

287

the soul and give up obeying common sense'. This is already the Sentence Vaticane 77, in which Epicurus opposes thinking for oneself (eautô) and thinking for Greece (Helladè). It is already Kant: thinking for oneself (leaving the status of being a minor) breaks off from collective thinking, from the mythical hallucination of subjects. If through the acquisition of language on the lips of his mother, the ego, the speaker, is already the national crowd, in the final analysis there is no longer an ego, no longer a crowd, no longer a nation, no longer a species, but an animal that is hemi-sexuated, atheist, without identity, defamilialized, defamiliarized, solitary, more silent, become once again a little wild, its ears perked more, a little staggering, a little erratic.

But Jesus of Nazareth's argument, which unfortunately had no effect on Christianity, is perhaps even deeper; it is surely deeper than Sextus Empiricus' rhetorical invention; it is even deeper than the completely extraordinary opposition, which Epicurus is the first philosopher to have put forward, between two kinds of (silent and linguistic) noeses; it goes right to the 'bottom' of the matter; it is radical.

It is at the heart of art.

It does not mean merely consenting to not knowing what one is unsure of; it means also refusing to obey any social representation, any political tyranny, any religious prophecy.

*

Do not distinguish between humans and inhumans. Do not draw a sharp line between city dwellers (polis) and the city-less (apolis).

*

The version of Jesus' Nolite judicare is different in Luke 6:37, in which the text adds an implication:

'Nolite judicare et non condemnabimini.' 'Judge not, and ye shall not be judged.' Judgement is called krisis in Greek—crisis. If you do not enter the world of judgement, you will not enter the world of exclusion and damnation. Give. Give more if someone wounds you. Creation is a pure gift. A true gift is a gift without an ulterior motive. Don't seek out looks from others. Don't look back at any look. Move forward. Ekstasis defines the movement of going out of oneself. (Ek-stasis, still more precisely, means to leave behind the stasis. It means leaving behind the civil war.) Moreover, in the text, at the very moment when Jesus says 'Suspend judgement! Abandon the crisis!', he has just written silently on the earth.

Se inclinans digito scribebat in terra.

But Jesus, in that he had stooped down, was writing with his finger in the dust of the ground.

This is the only time when God writes.

*

Epekhô in Pyrrho's mouth: I suspend my judgement, I persist in the in-finite, a-oristic aporia.

Epekhô in Husserl's mouth: I switch off my belief in the world, I momentarily put in parentheses not only history, but time.

Epekhô in Jesus' mouth: I stop obeying. I leave the pack, I write.

CHAPTER 98

Rousseau's beautiful letter about anchoritism, dating to 1762, begins with these lines: I was born with a natural love for solitude. Society, for which my imagination pays the price in my retreat, ends up making all the societies whom I have left disgust me. You suppose that I am unhappy and eaten away by melancholy. Oh, Monsieur! How wrong you are! It's in Paris that I was like that, etc.

But in contrast to so much beauty, I perhaps prefer D'Alembert's level-headed sentence: All the circumstances that are essential to my happiness are not in the power of the power.

*

I believed that it was for values that were opposed to those which were in current use around me that I suddenly resigned from all the activities that I was engaged in up to then: but it was probably *my life's goal*. Collective human domestication is exhausting, deafening. It consists of an unflagging dialogue, of solicited agglutination, of prescribed significations, of unbearable prohibitions, of meaningless admonishments. Abandoning a mission is to 'de-mission', to resign. Leaving behind a domos is to 'de-domesticate one-self'. To be an apolis, a city-less person, is to leave behind the city and not to drag anyone else along.

It means to recover a little silence.

One must not expect the deserter to have a general's vantage point.

One must rush towards what one likes best without sensing the need to judge it.

Read like men and women of letters. Approach the earth as if one were going to die.

As free as cats.

And as mute as the stones to which they go, where they leap, where they paw themselves, where they warm themselves in the sunray that makes colour and falls.

CHAPTER 99

Erebus

The moon was casting a feeble light on the different State bodies that were represented. The old president, with his livid face, his tense hand on the cloth of my suit jacket, was tugging me by the arm. One could make out bits of stripes, copper barrettes, naked throats, naked wrists, silk blouses or stoles, eyes, never whole faces. The laughter, the voices, were noisy in the presidential garden. The moonlight was disincarnating the bodies that were giving out these voices. It was stretching the walls of the enclosure, widening the very plates that were passing by. The trays of crabs became soft and whitish. Little hors-d'oeuvres dishes bulging with the stringy flesh of lobsters. The light was dimming. Those dilated bodies were feeble. We were at the end of the world. It was the Élysée Palace, the Elysium.

Erstwhile, Night was embraced by Chaos. She had a son whom she called Erebus. He was cast into Hades, where he became a vast, slow, sad, dark river with swampy banks. One must imagine a little grey house on the bank of this river. A boat lashed to an iron stake. This is where I found a place to live.

I was alive.

The rejection of the elites had come back in fashion.

Abbeys needed to be refounded on mountain slopes. Islands needed to be sought out once again in the sea. War had gone from being revolutionary to becoming mercantile again. Its motives, from being civil, had become religious once again. The confrontation, from being planetary, could now no longer be localized. Ever since the First World War, rare had become the deaths among the warriors who had confronted each other with fifes and drums, brandishing flags, rushing towards their horses, finding themselves face to face on a battlefield.

The States fired off their last cannons.

The former wild-animal-like predation again tried out its blows, it solitary combats, its complicated murders, its crazy flesh-eating excitation.

The last human beings were back. They stood alone, at the edge of what remains of nature, in the suburbs, on remote shores, concealed among bushes, steering clear of bands of cats gone wild, of runaways, of wolf-children, of haggard people.

*

Haggard was an erstwhile hunting term. A haggard was a hawk that had lived in the wilds for at least one year before being captured. By speaking of a haggard hawk, hunters evoked that paradoxical state of a hawk in livery, after its moulting, whose domestication was no longer really possible and yet whose wildness was lost.

Haggard is the bird of prey from which one can expect, in the best cases, no more than a temporary capitulation, which a starvation diet excessively alarms before the predation to which it is suddenly exposed, which hooding throws it into a panic because of the artificial night engulfing its head.

*

Seneca the Son had written: Redeo inhumanior quia inter homines fui. I come home more inhuman because I have gone among humans.

Literally: I come back more inhuman because, among men, I was.

*

Ovid, Antelme, the purest, the greatest, thought this: Men are no humans.

More or less human are men.

CHAPTER 100

My name is Louise Michel, captain of the Francs-Tireuses (the women irregular soldiers), member of the Society of Free Thinkers, of the Club of the Revolution, of the Rights of Women, and of the Garibaldi Legion. I am among those human beings who prefer that one calls the things that they refer to by the names that define them. Galley slaveries for the commissariats. Thieveries for the banks. Slaughterhouses for the courtrooms. Cemeteries for the maternity hospitals. Maternity hospitals for the graves. The municipal service department needs to change the signs that one finds at the bottom of staircases in the town halls.

*

Louise Michel: Everything was grandiose in the Commune, to the extent that the balance of power was unfavourable for us. With their dogs, the Versaillais chased after the Communists all the way into the graves. In the light of May, Paris was like a sepulchre in which it seems to me, however, that I never felt afraid. The air on the hill of Montmartre was full of little bits of burnt paper that fluttered, along with the first delicate grape leaves, around our faces.

*

Louise Michel wrote in 1871: Once one defends a cause with weapons, one experiences the struggle so completely that one is no longer any more of oneself than a projectile.

*

Paul Lafargue, Karl Marx's son-in-law, arriving from London, interviewed Louise Michel for the newspaper *Le Socialiste*.

Louise Michel:

'But why are you weeping, Monsieur Lafargue?'

'I didn't expect to see you behind a grill, Mademoiselle. I had hoped to talk with a socialist militant surrounded by her comrades in a heated room.'

'My dear Lafargue, blow your nose! There is no heated parlour in this hotel where the bourgeois lodge me gratis.'

'Your health isn't good enough to say behind bars. The comrades are going to make a petition so that you will be given a pardon.'

'Instead of demanding a pardon, which I will refuse from the Prefect of the Seine, bring me books. I would like to read Darwin's *The Descent of Man*. It will fortify my English.'

*

To Clemenceau and to Marboeuf who came to visit her in her cell:

'Please understand me, Messieurs. I like being in prison. I like to read. In all cases, one spends one's life in a cage. One has the impression of never ceasing for an instant to file down the bars of one's cage in order to find oneself in a bigger cell. Of course, it gets larger every time, but it is not the space itself. I like to be alone, I like to read, I like to learn, I like to study, I like to write. Once the jail door closes on me, my anguish vanishes. In prison, my thoughts are free. Money worries no longer trouble me. I wish never to receive a pardon any more. Ever since my mother has died, I no longer have worries about her sadness when she knew that I was under lock and key. I intend to accept only an armistice for all of us, or nothing.'

*

Louise Michel's letter addressed to the Prefect of Police on 28 December 1885: 'Stop bothering me with my pardon. You should have the honesty to leave me alone in the prison where you have put me without asking for my opinion.'

Telegram from the Director of Saint-Lazare Prison, addressed to the Prefect of Polis on 14 January 1886: 'Mademoiselle Michel refuses to leave the establishment. What can we do?'

The Prefect of Police: 'Mademoiselle Michel should be led by force outside of the establishment in which she is detained.'

The police captain put in charge of the release was forced to pay with his own money a fiacre, which he let inside the prison.

He put Louise Michel, screaming and with her hands tied in front of her, into the fiacre.

The horse began to bray.

Everyone was shouting.

The captain closed the fiacre door with a padlock, sat down on the other side, personally conducted Louise Michel to 89 route d'Asnières, in Levallois-Perret, where a municipal councillor, Monsieur Charles Moïse, had a small flat prepared for her, with its rent paid by Monsieur Félicien Marboeuf.

The police captain did not untie her hands until she had entered the flat.

Louise Michel rubbed her wrists with satisfaction while Charles Moïse showed her around her new domicile.

The two-room flat was furnished tastefully: a finely carved Japanese wardrobe from Nagasaki, a Catalan wicker armchair made in Canyamel, an empty bookcase.

Mademoiselle Michel told the police captain several times that she was very happy with the flat that Monsieur Marboeuf had rented for her.

On the marble fireplace mantel there was a Pompon-Vidert horse in resin.

The report of the police captain in charge of the extraction, to the Prefect of Police: 'It is more difficult to bring Louise Michel out of prison in that she makes no difficulties about remaining detained there.'

CHAPTER 101

De solitudine

Who speaks of dead horses? I am like Montaigne returning to Montaigne. I am like Paul, become blind, finding himself like a horse on its back, with his four horseshoes in the air, on the road to Damascus. In three steps. A light that unsaddles, sudden blinding, a new light.

The mere occlusion of the eyelids can make what vision does not show surge forth in this world.

Sometimes light must be replaced by a candle. De occulte vivendo. It does not break the night. What is a stake is to join the hidden, desiring, unappeased, deep life.

Such is the way. It is the path to the origin.

The origin gains ground in the world.

Time extends.

Light becomes more and more incandescent in the depths of dark space.

The mortals see red, that is, they begin to see without a screen.

The bottom of the earth is boiling red iron.

*

The originary lava sometimes escapes from the soul, sometimes at mountain peaks that suddenly tear apart, sometimes in the depths of space where the dense, pre-explosive wandering of time itself is nestled.

In 2003, V838 Monocerotis, a red star, successively swallowed three planets orbiting around it.

*

Culture has never been autonomous in regard to nature. Euripides the Tragedian wrote: Civilization does not separate itself from bestial life (thériôdès bios). There is no autonomy of life in regard to the matter that spurts out into space and falls back in an ellipse. There is no meta-language, no meta-polis, no meta-chrony. There is no autonomy of all the kinds of languages cried out by animal species at dawn in regard to the sun that rises from the lowest part of the sky. There is no autonomy of human beings, nor of wild animals, nor of flowers, nor of the clouds that make the light alternate, nor of the shadows that they bring over the fields or the sand or the water. There remains a steep fault line. I part company with the neo-stoicism of the ancient Romans at the beginning of the Empire, a philosophy which constitutes the foundation of Western ideology—which also formed the basis of Christianity—in that, between what lives and the physical milieu in which it lives, the exchanges are numerous; non evolutional continuity exists. Inanimate beings, stars, crystals and minerals evolve with the physical space in which their singular forms are caught. Living beings are separated from their environment by the gradual deployment of their disjoint, dissident, lateral, necrosanct, arborescent evolution. Bees, ferns, human beings, frogs and ants contribute to strange contemporaneity that is, however, without synchrony. There is an insane, non-rational, pre-linguistic continuity in the discontinuation of seasons and ages, of births and deaths, in the fragmentation of cells, in the fissiparousness of elementary forms. Moreover, to morphological evolution (what one calls space) and to individual evolution (what one calls life), must be added the evolution that results in the acts of the actuality (what one calls time). What is born is a curious withdrawal: a withdrawal with respect to the sexual scene, to the original body, to one's environment; a withdrawal vis-à-vis to one's family, and to the history of one' ancestors.

Withdrawal.

He withdraws.

This is how anchoritism is founded.

One must understand the truth that is characteristic of modern times: Everything is broken. 'Old Europe' no longer exists. There is what remains of the 1945 occupation zones; the remains of fascism; the rather bipolar fragments of the two empires that had divided up the world; the relics of the most terrible theocracy that the world has known (Christianity). I have never left the ruins of Le Havre where

I would walk, as a child, pushing my head against the force of the wind to arrive in the makeshift huts where the lower-grade classes of the boy's lycée took place.

Goebbels' phrase: Ein Volk, ein Reich, ein Führer. For reasons that stemmed from my family, my moral philosophy found itself imprisoned just as soon. Neither nation, nor society, nor dependence.

It was two years before the Second World War, in 1938, in Vienna, when the acclamation 'Ein Volk, ein Reich, ein Führer' was chanted for the first time in Europe.

*

I had studied in the classes of my mentor, Emmanuel Levinas, before the month of May 1968, in the new university of Nanterre-La-Folie. I then took cats and the state of the sky for a mentor.

Culture must not *finish off* the construction of the world. One must let life be the master of the fate of the earth. In a vacant lot, the vegetation is freer than in the forest itself; light is more vivid; the weight of the past constrains less; one must let time lift History.

Two freedoms must be distinguished.

The freedom characteristic of the élan that carries matter, characteristic of the untameable, the uneducable, the wild.

Freedom as emancipation from domestication.

Two freedoms. I am optimistic to the point of delirium. I believe that if one cannot destroy the acquisition of the national language, one can rip its fabric a little. I believe that if one cannot tear oneself entirely away from the guilt that is born from 'the prohibition' handed over to each of us by our elders, one can rework one's anguish into excitation. I believe that if one cannot be free, one can move away from one's family, reach the periphery of the group, lessen the servitude, make it less voluntary. That if one cannot free oneself from obeying the first world and childhood, one can undo the knots and make them much looser than one supposes, between all the bonds that twist and strangle. That if one cannot tear reflection from hallucination, one can detach thought from the contents of dreaming. That if one cannot release the brain from the spell cast by all of its beliefs and magic practices, one can withdraw from gods and remain remote from their temples. That if one cannot remove the soul from orbiting around its sun of repetition and reproduction, not only mutiny is conceivable, but one can also desert. That if one cannot wean the desire for one's absent close ones and one's models and one's simulacrums and one's follies, one can defalsify the false, one can bring forward a little light into the night—a light that projects, from itself, a still darker shadow, a brand new shadow, a darkness that one suffers less from, a magnificent shadow surging forth ever more.

*

A light comparable to the first solar light that makes one stare wide-eyed when one emerges into this world during the fundamental fright of the originary distress.

*

A light in which to read.

Sigmund Freud said that the meditative reading of a book was the only positive contribution that human beings had found during the redoubtable process of civilization.

*

Human society: resemblance to death.

The anchorite of letters: live dissemblance.

*

I exist, but less that one believes, you more, he is dead, lies to us.

CHAPTER 102

A woman was singing in a low voice. The sheet music had been placed on the grand piano from which the cover had not been raised above the sounding board. The French window had been opened onto the meadow. On the cushion of the French window, a cat was sleeping. In the distance, in the lower part of the meadow, at the end of the meadow, the horses were grazing near a path along the stream.

The sun was setting.

The singing was freeing itself little by little from the melody that had been noted down, the tempo became slower. Suddenly the woman started singing in strange trills, marvellous trills.

The music brought back, with the pain, a kind of peace.

*

Something, from trill to trill, swirled ever-more slowly, staggering, cradling.

*

Later, when night had fallen, the woman was still reading her music. She had lit the little curved lamp on the piano.

She was still singing to herself. She was standing. She was bending over the sheet music. Her hair was caught in the light.

He had arrived late. He had sat down in front of her, on the sofa. He had just served himself a glass of wine. He was listening to her.

As for her, she was keeping the beat with her hand. Her hand would move forward into the halo of the lamp and would mark each beat, as it dropped. The song was inexpressibly sad.

She pulled the curved lamp towards her to focus it on the lied cycle itself. To read better. To sing better. Not much more light could be seen in the room.

He was cold. He stood up and, making the least noise possible, headed for the open French window. He was going to close the two panes when he saw, very close to him, the head of a horse. The horse had come all the way up from the end of the meadow and was softly dancing. Its legs were dancing more slowly than the measure, without keeping time, but dancing. The horse raised its head, turned towards him, looking at him with its big sad eyes. They looked at each other in silence. Then the man left the French window open. He leant against the window frame and both of them, the horse, the man, next to each other, listened to the song. Both of them watched the woman leaning over, her chignon caught in the tiny light of the lamp, above the notes that she was deciphering, that she was singing.

The title *Les Désarçonnés* and the ways that the verb *désarçonner* and the noun *arçon* are used in puns and allusions throughout the book are impossible to duplicate fully in English. The word *arçon* means a (horse riding) 'tree', that is a wooden frame used in the construction of a saddle. By extension in French, the word is associated with *selle* (saddle). The verb *désarçonner* means to remove from the *arçon* and thus to be 'unsaddled', 'thrown' off the saddle (while riding), 'unseated', 'unhorsed'. Figuratively, the French verb means 'to be (completely) baffled', to be (completely) 'thrown', as in the example: Sa réponse me désarçonna (I was completely thrown by his reply). The English title *The Unsaddled* should thus be taken literally as well as figuratively.

I have adopted Chris Turner's solution of 'the Erstwhile' for Quignard's key word and concept *le Jadis*, as explained in his translator's note to *The Sexual Night* (Seagull Books, 2014, p. 158) and in Quignard's text itself in that book: 'In Old French, *jadis* breaks down into *a ja y a dies*—already there was a day. In Modern English we should unpack this almost incomprehensible sequence—Already, in the past, there was there is.'